THROUGH

TO

YOU

EMILY HAINSWORTH

BALZER + BRAY
An Imprint of HarperCollins*Publishers*

Balzer + Bray is an imprint of HarperCollins Publishers.

Through to You

Copyright © 2012 by Emily Hainsworth

Library of Congress Cataloging-in-Publication Data
Hainsworth, Emily.
Through to you / Emily Hainsworth. — 1st ed.
p. cm.
Summary: "When a teen boy loses the love of his life in a car
accident, he'll do anything to get her back—even travel to another
universe."—Provided by publisher.
ISBN 978-0-06-209420-9
[1. Grief—Fiction. 2. Love—Fiction. 3. Fantasy.] I. Title.
PZ7.H128163Th 2012   2012006549
[Fic]—dc23   CIP
                                                            AC

Typography by Torborg Davern
13 14 15 16 17 CG/RRDH 10 9 8 7 6 5 4 3 2 1
❖
First paperback edition, 2014

To Stefan, for showing me another world,
and to Courtney,
for helping me find my way there

I need to look great for all patrons,

so please keep me away from

food, drinks, pets, ink, pencils,

and other things that may harm

For this is Wisdom; to love, to live,
To take what Fate, or the Gods, may give,
To ask no question, to make no prayer,
To kiss the lips and caress the hair,
Speed passion's ebb as you greet its flow,—
To have,—to hold,—and,—in time,—let go!

—Laurence Hope, "THE TEAK FOREST"

ONE

IT'S THE SAME DREAM I'VE BEEN HAVING FOR THE PAST TWO months—Viv walking away from glass and fire, her laughter echoing through the night. She's coming toward me, her lips stretched into a seductive smile. Her hips sway and I want to touch her so much it hurts. I want to bury my fingers in her black hair. She's a dark, stunning contrast to the bright flames rising behind her. I anticipate breathing in her scent—it's like spring— and running my hands over her skin, never letting go. But then she stops and looks away from me. The fire dances on her cheek. I want to scream, but I am mute. I reach for her, but I can't move. She turns back toward the flames.

I've lost her again.

I close my hand into a fist and I crack one eye open. Mike Liu stands at the end of the library table, uncomfortable.

"Hey, Cam. The bell rang."

I wipe drool from my mouth and peel my face off the spiral notebook in front of me. I rub at the deep ridges it leaves in my cheek. "Thanks."

He hesitates, adjusting the backpack on his shoulder. "See you at lunch?"

I don't look up. "Yeah."

As he walks away, I wish for a second I'd said more than two words to him. But two words are all I manage to give anyone these days.

Other students filter out of the library. I'm alone.

I slump back in my chair and stare out the window. It has a good view of the street corner. I stare at it until something sweeps by the glass—a tangle of black hair. I stand up too fast, nearly knocking the chair over. My legs freeze; I blink, and it's just a raven flying by. I exhale. Viv has been dead for two long months, but she's still everywhere.

And nowhere.

Outside it's too warm for early October. Indian summer. The leaves are still hanging on to the trees, flowers are still blooming. Everything is so *alive*. I wish winter would hurry and freeze it all. I'm supposed to be in trig, but I make a beeline for her corner. I changed my schedule so I could see this wedge of concrete from every class. By all appearances, it's an average intersection where two sidewalks meet. The old utility pole that snapped in two has been replaced, the landscaping patched back together. The cards, pictures, and drooping stuffed animals are even beginning to blend in. The flowers I brought this week have wilted.

It's been two months exactly. Today.

Tonight.

I try not to look at the smiling photographs, but one of them catches my eye, taken straight out of the yearbook. It's from freshman year, when she was still cheerleading. Her curves didn't quite fill out her uniform then. She wears red and white ribbons in her hair. Her cheeks are pink and healthy, her smile even wider than I remember. I force my eyes to the notes, though I've memorized them all.

Viv, you are missed

Why do bad things happen to good people? Miss you, Viv

Can't believe you're gone

I dig my fingernails into my palms. They don't *miss* her. I recognize every one of the signed names. None of them would have called her their friend to her face. You're not supposed to opt out of the popular crowd like she did. Either you're never in, or you fall from it, like me.

I need a cigarette.

There's a pack at the bottom of my bag, and I rifle through notebooks and loose papers searching for it. My fingers graze cellophane and I withdraw the half-crumpled box, tapping it against

3

my palm. I flip back the lid, place a cigarette between my lips, and fumble for a lighter. My pockets are cluttered, and I get annoyed when I don't immediately find one. I pull the bag off my shoulder and dig through it until I notice a slight bulge in the lining—eureka. There's a small tear that I hastily widen, itching to light up, but when I pull my hand out and see my Zippo instead of the cheap Bic I was looking for, I stop.

My thumb traces over the monogram she had engraved on it for my seventeenth birthday—C.P. I close my fist so I won't have to look at it, but the *feel* of it is worse. Cold, smooth, and hard. My knuckles turn white. Before I can think, I chuck it into the semi-mangled shrubs where Viv's front tire came to rest. I'm sure that's the spot, because when I woke up next to her lifeless body, covered in glass and smelling of gasoline, I stumbled around the car and *fell* into those bushes. They were prickly and unforgiving, and I found scratches under my shirt days later. I don't remember much of that night besides her bloody shape slumped against the cracked driver's-side window, but I remember those fucking bushes.

If I hadn't dropped the stupid lighter—if Viv hadn't laughed at me for being a klutz and reached for it herself—if she hadn't been going quite so fast so we could get to my house and into bed—and if it hadn't been raining—I might not be standing here staring at her pathetic shrine on the sidewalk.

I wish it were mine.

Stupid fucking lighter.

Coming here was a bad idea. It always is.

I'm brushing past the utility pole when I hear a voice over my shoulder.

"Cam?"

I turn, but no one's there.

I turn again, all the way around, and I see no one, but I could swear a girl said my name. The voice had a metallic quality, as if spoken through a spinning fan blade.

"Mr. Pike." A deep new tone takes me by surprise. I whirl around to see Coach Reed—*Mr. Reed*—the vice principal of Fowler High. He gives me this assessing look as he approaches, the one where you're supposed to feel like he can see inside your very soul. It hasn't worked on me since I quit the team.

"Pike, you're standing on school grounds."

I wait for the punch line.

He plucks the cigarette from my mouth and hands it to me. Shit.

"Even if you were eighteen, smoking on school grounds *is* prohibited." He gestures across the street to the graffitied bus shelter, where the smokers of Fowler High seek refuge, kids and teachers alike. "If you're going to cultivate the habit, do it *off* campus."

I stare at the bench under the shelter, at the beat-up safety glass that's so scratched it doesn't qualify as a window anymore. I look back to Viv's shrine, to the cards, the bushes, the utility pole. You wouldn't be able to see any of it through that glass. I look down at the unlit cigarette in my hand. Did I think I would have enjoyed it without her? I toss it into the gutter.

"Just quit, sir."

What do you know—three words. I walk away before Mr. Reed—I will not call him Coach—has time to answer. I can *feel* his concern. Since I'm supposed to be in trigonometry, I stroll back toward school, pulling open a beaten metal door down the hall from the art room. He calls out to me.

"Camden—"

I throw the half-smoked pack of cigarettes into a trash can before the door clicks shut behind me.

The cafeteria overflows into the main hall, as usual. Budget cuts or bake sale mismanagement have forced the school to *maximize space* rather than expand. The sad thing is, almost everyone prefers eating out here in the dim, outdated hallway than eating at the tables in a brightly lit room that reeks of stale pizza. Almost everyone, including me.

There are alcoves along the wall for the numerous double doors leading into the auditorium, and the doorways are always hot property because they're more private, but I snag one early. Two girls glance over when I sit down. They go quiet, and I can feel one of them staring at me. I sit cross-legged and don't look up. The other one mutters and I hear them zipping their backpacks. I relax a little—they're going to move.

But then one of them comes and kneels by me.

"Hi . . ." She's a redhead with a heart-shaped face. I don't recognize her. Probably a freshman or sophomore who doesn't know any better. I turn my head and don't acknowledge her. She continues softly, "I just wanted to say . . . I'm sorry. I didn't know her, but it's really sad. She was so pretty."

My hair hangs in my eyes. I don't look up, don't even act like she's there.

She stays next to me for an awkward half minute, waiting for me to respond while I study the floor tiles and wish people would stop trying to pretend they care. Finally, she gets the message. She quietly picks up her bag and joins her friend again.

"See?" the other girl says. "Now do you believe me?"

They walk away down the hall. I exhale.

I don't eat. Viv and I used to leave for lunch, or at least go outside to smoke. I was just assigned a book for English, so I take it out of my backpack. I don't know what the story's about, but people are way less likely to talk to you if you look busy. There are no windows in the hall, and the cafeteria faces the athletic field. This is the only part of the day when I can't see the street corner. I keep the book open and try to disappear in my alcove, waiting for the period to end. The lunch voices meld into chaotic chatter around me.

I'm dozing off when a backpack thuds down beside me. Mike. I forgot he said something about meeting for lunch. I return to the book and try to look like I'm really into it until I notice I'm holding it upside down. Mike notices too, but he pulls out a sketchbook and doesn't say anything.

An obnoxious set of voices breaks through the lunch hum, drawing my attention from the upside-down book. Logan West and Sharif Rahman lead a group of my former teammates; they're pushing their way down the hall.

Sharif hollers at Mike, "Hey, Liu!"

"Rahman," Mike returns. "What's up?"

"Hey, Pike!" Logan shouts at me. He flips me off.

I look away. If Viv were in the alcove with me, I wouldn't have even seen him.

After they're gone, I don't move. Mike is absently sketching. He takes out an energy bar and starts to chew. I can't believe he still eats those things. I wouldn't play a game without them once upon a time, but they taste like chocolate sawdust. He leans back into the shadows of the alcove, chewing while he draws, and it's all I can do to sit there with him not saying anything.

"Look, Cam—" he says suddenly. "Is there anything I can do?"

I straighten. "I'm fine."

He puts down his pencil and gives me a sidelong glance. The kind he used to give me if I called a bad play. I tense up, and he sees it. "I just—I see you out there on the corner all the time. It isn't healthy, man."

This is what separates Mike from those other guys walking away down the hall: He's the only one I stayed friends with— who stayed friends with *me*.

And right now, I hate him for it.

"I'm fine. I'll be fine," I repeat.

Mike shakes his head. His voice gets low. "Have you thought about maybe taking down the things outside? The notes and stuff?"

I raise my head and really make eye contact for the first time.

He takes one look at my face and starts backpedaling.

"I just thought— Maybe it isn't helping?"

I clench my teeth. We'll both regret it if I open my mouth now. I pick up my backpack and head away down the hall. The bell rings and the space around me floods with people pressing in on me. I shove my way back to my locker at the other end of the building to get my history book for fifth period. When I finally get there, I mess up the combination twice and have to mouth the numbers to myself to get them right.

17 . . . 08 . . . 31.

On the third attempt, I lift the latch, and my locker swings open. *World History II* sits atop the stack of books at the bottom. Just as I reach to get it, a large hand flashes out and slams the door shut again. The meaty fingers stay splayed over the metal in front of my face. French-fry breath is hot on my neck. I turn and stare into Logan's flared nostrils. He reminds me of a bull, and I'm standing between him and a bank of red lockers. His arm blocks my escape. He stares me down, tight-lipped and unblinking. His blond hair is spiked into daggers. I look away. Two years ago, I might have been him. Two months ago, I wouldn't have cared. He laughs and high-fives Sharif over my head. I watch them leave. Logan jumps to touch the ceiling halfway down the corridor. They move down the emptying hall like they own it.

I abandon my locker, ignoring the bell as I head back through the halls. I don't even glance at the secretaries in the main office as I walk out the front doors, away from the whole fucking school.

TWO

MY HOUSE IS EMPTY. I WANDER THROUGH THE ROOMS, UNSURE OF
where I want to be until I realize I don't want to be anywhere.
Every room has a hole in it—where a chair was, a stereo, a set of
books, a closet of clothes. Mom never filled them in after Dad
left, and I guess I didn't care. But since the accident, all I can see
are the holes in things.

I end up in the kitchen. Open the refrigerator, stare into it,
close it. Finally, I read the note in the fruit bowl, wedged with
some cash between a too-soft pear and a brown banana. Mom
hasn't learned to text, so the fruit bowl is our courier.

Cam—
Don't forget your appt. with Dr. Summers again.

Late tonight. Here's money for pizza.
Love,
Mom

I count the cash and stick it in my pocket. She's never changed the amount. Still enough here for me *and* Viv. I stare at the number for the pizza place on the fridge. It's called Pizza Emergency, and they actually deliver pizzas in an old converted ambulance. Viv used to think that was hysterical. She'd call up and say, *You've got to help us—we need pepperoni, STAT!*

We both laughed at the dumb joke every time, but now all I can picture is the broken pole on the street corner and an ambulance driving slowly away, with its lights off.

I walk to my room, fall on the bed, and sleep.

I have the dream of Viv again. I'm almost thankful for it. She looks so beautiful, so carefree. Only this time something's different. She's still walking toward me, away from the flames . . . but I can't hear her. Everything is silent.

She gets to that place by the pole where she always stops, but there's still no sound. I see the look in her dark eyes, the light of flames dancing on her cheek—and then I hear a voice. But it isn't hers. It's metallic.

"Cam? Camden!"

I wake up reaching for her and she isn't there. I'm alone in my bed. I bury my head beneath my pillow and hate everything, whisper every impossible thing I've wished for since that night in August. All I get is a damp pillow. When I feel like my eyes are going to swell shut, I walk blindly to the bathroom and stand under the shower. I let cold water force my eyes open, numbing my skin until it isn't burning with longing.

I don't realize I'm still in my clothes until I shut the water off.

Dr. Summers's office is located in the basement of her split-level house, ten blocks over from mine. Her golden retriever, Lance, meets me at the door, wagging his tail. The office is furnished with two incredibly soft leather couches and a rolling desk chair. The carpet is beige. Pictures of her husband and son dot the walls.

Right away, I can tell something's up. Dr. Summers doesn't sit in the chair like she always does. She perches casually on the other couch, resting her elbow on the arm. Her clipboard is in her lap. Her short, fading-blond hair is still tucked neatly in place, but her glasses are next to her on the table, and she studies me with careful eyes.

"It's been a couple weeks since I saw you, Cam." Her smile stays in place. "How are things going?"

"Sorry, I forgot last week."

This is such a shitty lie, I'm embarrassed. I've been coming here every Friday at four o'clock for the past two years, since I quit the team. Since my dad took off. She knows how I feel about him, about football, and about people at school. I've always told her the truth about things, but each week for the past two months, I've been telling her lies. I don't *want* her to know how I really

12

feel about Viv. I mean, she knows how I felt before, but I can't tell her what goes through my head these days. That my life ended when Viv's did. That the accident was my fault. That every day I wake up and wonder why I'm the one still here.

Lance shoves his nose under the door, and I glance over.

Dr. Summers sees this, and her face brightens.

"You know, I'm going to break my own rule. Let's let Lance in, just for today."

Before I can say anything, she opens the door and the dog runs into the room like he's just won a jackpot. He plants himself on my feet, tail wagging furiously, and stares up at my face with his tongue lolling out. I glance at Dr. Summers, who is back on the other couch. She nods, and I pet her dog's head, because how could I not with him looking at me that way?

"It's a good day for *you*," I whisper into his ear.

Dr. Summers leans forward. "But not a good one for you?"

I shut my mouth, look from her to her dog, and see how perfectly she set that up.

"No," I say, defeated.

"It's been two months today, hasn't it?"

I don't say anything.

"How do you feel about that, Cam?"

I grit my teeth. I have bunches of Lance's reddish fur squeezed into both my fists. I loosen my grip and pet him normally. He looks at me with huge brown eyes and licks my arm.

"You've been trying so hard *not* to talk about Viv since she died . . ."

My eyes sting. I stare into nothingness and bite hard on the inside of my cheek. I've never cried here and I'm not about to start. I'm almost positive she knows I've been lying to her, which makes this even worse. Lance rolls over for a tummy rub.

"Cam," she says gently, "I'm here to listen."

I focus on Lance, skimming my fingers over the soft gold hairs on his belly. I feel her watching me, waiting for me to speak. I can't stand it.

"I have this dream—about Viv," I say. Dr. Summers's shoulders relax, and I know this will be enough, for now. "I keep having it, over and over, where she's coming toward me, but then she turns away. . . ."

She talks about what the dream might mean to me. I sort of listen. It's mostly psycho-babble, but I have to seem interested or I'll never get out of here. By five o'clock, I'm exhausted, but it's worth it because Dr. Summers looks pleased when she walks me to the door.

"Thank you for sharing the dream with me, Cam." She squeezes my shoulder. "I know you're in a lot of pain, and it's *normal* for you to feel that way . . . but I also think Viv wouldn't want you to go on like this forever."

I'm petting Lance on the head, but my hand halts on his ear. "What do you mean?"

"Just that *you* still have so much life to live . . ."

"And Viv doesn't?" I say flatly.

Dr. Summers pauses. "That's not what I mean—"

"What then, you want me to forget her?" My skin prickles.

"No, nothing like that . . ." she says. "I just think Viv would want what's best—"

"How do you know what she'd want? You never even met her!"

The dog tries to lick my hand, but I pull away and slam the door behind me. I can't believe my shrink tried to put words in my dead girlfriend's mouth. I storm down the sidewalk for one block, then another, but pretty soon my bad leg twinges and then my eyes start to burn. I slow to my normal pace, trying to remember how to breathe—on my own. I can't even figure out what to do next, where to go. I close my eyes and try to think what Viv would want. If she were here, she'd tell me . . . I'd know.

THREE

FALL MIGHT MAKE AN APPEARANCE AFTER ALL THIS YEAR. I WANDER around town for hours but find myself on the corner again. I wish I'd brought a jacket. It's eleven o'clock, almost exactly the time it happened. The moon is bright in the sky, illuminating the pictures of Viv, and I can't tear my eyes away. It's just a cluster of plastic-sheathed photographs, but in them she looks *alive*. They make her feel real, like she's only out of town, and when she gets back, this will all have been a dream. A nightmare.

I stand in front of the utility pole, arms locked around my torso. With my luck, Reed will show up to chastise me for being on school grounds after hours, but I had to come. I don't really know why two months should matter so much, but I guess that's like asking why every second that's passed since that awful night matters. There's a large rock at the edge of the bushes that I sit on and shiver. If Viv were here, we'd share a cigarette and put our hands inside each other's clothes to keep warm. I smile at this, lose myself in the thought of her skin . . . until I realize if Viv were here, we wouldn't *be* shivering on this stupid corner. I press my palms against my eyes.

Tires squeal in the distance, and I look up to see headlights streaking down the road. The car turns the corner, running the red light. They swerve into the wrong lane and they're pointed right at me. Someone shrieks. I close my eyes. A breeze gusts across my face, exhaust rushes into my nose . . .

The car accelerates through the rain. The light ahead is green. I place a cigarette between her lips, but the Zippo slips through my fingers, landing somewhere by her feet. She takes her hand off my thigh with an exasperated laugh and reaches for it—the light turns red. She slams on the brakes, I grab for the wheel—the rain slides sideways across the windshield. I never hear her scream.

I open my eyes. The taillights are small now, disappearing down the road. A beer can bounces three times across the pavement and comes to rest in the middle of the street before I exhale. Friday-night fun.

I lean against the pole, hidden by the shadow it casts in the moonlight. The wind picks up, needling through my clothes. The street is empty now, but I blink at the place where the car disappeared. I was hoping it would hit the pole and kill me, too.

What the fuck is wrong with me?

I pace back and forth in front of the teddy bears, notes, and dead flowers.

Maybe Mike was right . . . maybe I should take them down. A shrine won't bring her back. Or make the accident not my fault.

My body aches with memory. I'm desperate to talk to her. She'd understand how I feel—she always did. It used to be like we each knew what the other was thinking: I'd complete her sentences; she could anticipate my thoughts. I remember a time at the Coffee Haus when she stopped me in front of the counter and stared deep into my eyes. She turned to the barista and said very seriously, *Vanilla latte and a bagel*—like she could see inside my head. She filled in the gaps, made me feel so complete.

The only person in my head now is me.

"Cam?"

Viv?

I stop pacing and look back toward the pole. A new light cuts through the darkness beyond it. I squint at it, expecting to see another car, but it isn't headlights. This glow is different.

It's not coming toward me and it's not in the road.

"Cam!"

That voice again. I turn around—and around.

No one's there.

But I still see the glow. I take a few steps sideways, because the light looks like it's coming from behind the wooden pole. A fire? I approach it quickly, but when my jeans brush the bushes on the other side, I freeze. One by one the hairs stand straight on the back of my neck. There are no flames.

A green light glows behind the utility pole.

In it stands a girl.

A girl I can see *through.*

"Cam!"

Her skin, clothing, and hair are transparent and tinted green in the strange light. Through her body, I watch leaves on the bushes rustle in the wind.

I've lost my mind.

My stomach feels like it's digesting a cannonball, but I raise my gaze to her face, waiting for it to shape-shift into something demonic and horrifying, because I've seen more than enough horror movies to know this is what I should expect. She stays girl-shaped, for now, but she has an odd expression. There are streaks down her face—as if she's been crying.

This is definitely *not* Viv. I don't know who this is.

I panic, trying to decide what to do. The most obvious thing would be to run. . . . My left leg aches with the urge to pound pavement, but my right one disagrees. Injury always wins. For the moment, though, neither fight nor flight seems necessary.

She stands still, staring at me.

"Cam?"

I'm not sure how to respond to an apparition that knows my name, so I just nod.

She clasps her hands together and wipes her face. "Oh my God."

And then it hits me—I'm hallucinating. I've finally cracked. I reach for the phone in my pocket, ready to call Dr. Summers, but before I can think of how I'll explain this, the girl says something else that shocks me.

"Are—are you a ghost?"

I hesitate, and look her up and down. She's still transparent, still slightly green, but her clothes seem normal enough. She's got on boots and a short skirt with a jean jacket. Her hair falls straight around her shoulders. For good measure, I inspect my very opaque arm. Am *I* a ghost?

"Are *you*?" I say.

My hallucination bites her lip.

Why didn't I hallucinate Viv?

And then a new thought occurs to me: That car that drove by—maybe it didn't swerve in time. Could it have hit me? Am I dead? Did I get my wish after all?

And if I'm dead, where's Viv?

The wind whips my hair, slicing through the fabric of my shirt. I must be hallucinating. I'm too goddamn cold to be dead. I stamp my foot and shove my hands in my pockets. She just stands there, wiping at her face, not speaking.

"I *said*, are *you* a ghost?"

The girl's eyebrows knit together, which is disarming because she stands between me and the school, and I can see the art classroom window through her forehead.

Her lip quivers. She reaches into her pocket and holds something out to me. I take a step closer, think better of it—in case she *isn't* part of my brain—and squint. There's a metallic green rectangle in her palm. On the front, in block letters, it's engraved—*C.P.*

A ghost is holding the lighter I threw away this morning.

Holy shit.

"Cam—"

"Where did you get that?" I snap. "How do you even know my name?"

Her face crumples, and she covers her eyes with her hands.

I run. I don't even consider my old injury until I'm halfway down the street. All I can think is *go-go-GO, get away*—but can you even run from your own brain? Pain shoots through every bone in my right leg, and my muscles buckle to a stop. I clench my jaw so tightly the tendons in my neck compete in agony with my leg. I look back, terrified I'll see some ghost-girl vision coming down the road after me.

But I'm alone.

FOUR

TWO MONTHS, ONE DAY.

Halfway through my shift at Smith's grocery store Saturday, I give in and let myself think. Sleeping didn't make the memory of what I saw go away, and herding shopping carts is a shitty distraction for my brain. Every time I turn around, I half expect to see the girl—hear her voice. Maybe I was mistaken and she's a normal human being. Ghosts don't wear jean jackets. You'd hardly think that's what she was . . . except for the whole transparent-green thing. I try to stay focused on the shoppers, the parking lot, but my mind keeps leaping from the rows of plastic carts to what did or didn't happen on the corner last night.

Maybe none of it was real. It might have been a dream, except I'm walking with a limp today because my right leg aches—like I actually ran from something.

Or am I imagining the pain, too?

I wasn't prepared for the two-month anniversary, that's all. I try to forget there will be more anniversaries—three, four, five, six months, a year—one thing at a time. Dr. Summers says stress does weird things to people. She'll never leave me alone if she thinks I see ghosts and hear voices.

I could call Dad.

The thought catches me so off guard, I'm almost hit by a cart a lady shoves in my direction. As if he and I could even have a normal conversation.

I snake my earbuds up the collar of my jacket and crank the volume. No lyrics, just synth, drum, and bass. Everyone entering and exiting the grocery store walks in time to the drumming in my ears. No, I won't call. There's nothing to tell. I had another messed-up dream about the corner, like I have ever since Viv died, that's all. I'm not buckling now. I limp out to the farthest parking spaces, retrieve a cart marooned on a curb, and crash it into another basket.

I wouldn't call him even if the girl I saw *was* a ghost.

When I clock out of work, I don't head right home. I wander Fayetteville without any real destination, except I stay far from the corner and the school. My calf muscle is still sore, but walking will stretch it out. I go down First Avenue from the grocery store, past all the fast-food places and a couple of strip malls. Our local grease pit, Fast Break, reeks of chili fries even from the street. They're playing *Casablanca* at the Chez Artiste—the first place Viv and I kissed. She got a job there one summer because it was close to Smith's Grocery. She'd sneak me into the projection room when I got off work and we'd stuff ourselves with popcorn, making up dialogue for the foreign films instead of reading the subtitles. She used to stroke the nape of my neck during the credits to make me shiver, and I'd trace kisses over the arch of her brow just to hear her gasp.

Eventually I find myself heading away from the bright restaurants and shops, following the road up the highest hill around until the pavement runs out. The water tower stands there, sentinel over town. Its massive gray cylinder isn't a destination in itself, though there's plenty of colorful graffiti around the base proclaiming who's been here and when. The dirt lot just beneath it is the real draw. If you drive up here at sunset, the sky is spectacular—not that anyone spends that much time actually admiring the view. Viv and I came our fair share in her little blue car. It's one place no one bothered us because they had better things to do.

I hang back when I reach the edge of the lot. Saturday night it gets pretty full. Music pulses into the darkness from several vehicles. The windows are mostly rolled up, but every now and then I catch a murmur of voices, laughter . . . two voices for every car.

I have no right to be here.

My lungs feel like they're filling with quicksand. Without Viv, I'm a creepy guy lurking outside other people's cars while they make out. I can't do this; I don't remember how—to get out of bed, to live my life, to *breathe*. I listen to the laughter, the conversations, and imagine the things gasped too low to hear. Things I used to have, that somehow made me complete.

Something brushes my neck, and I almost fall backward down an embankment. I paw behind my head—turning around and around, looking for ghosts, hoping for Viv. But there's nothing there. I step back up to where I'd been standing, under a low branch. The naked twigs on the end reach out to touch my neck. I break them off—tear at the branch until it twists and bends, but that part is alive and doesn't give in.

The house is quiet. I lie with my eyes closed, but sunlight streams onto my pillow. I sit up, swing my right leg over the side of the bed, and rub the scar that runs from the top of my thigh over my knee. It still throbs. I close my eyes and try to remember if I dreamed, but if I did, it's blissfully forgotten. I'm starting to debate which is worse: the part of my life I spend awake, the part I spend in nightmares . . . or maybe the part when I can't tell the difference. I glance around at my bare walls, the pile of clothes next to my bed. My desk is still a mess, the chair still knocked over from when I came in last night. But *no one* else is here—real, imaginary, or dead.

The newspaper is spread all over the kitchen counter. The dishes are starting to pile up in the sink, and the dishwasher is beeping despite the fact that it hasn't been run since last week. I pull it open, close it, and the beeping stops.

There's a new note in the fruit bowl.

Cam—
Trial Monday, working all weekend.
I'll be at the office if you need me.
Sorry! Miss you. XOXO
Love,
Mom

I drop the note back into the fruit. Lawyers always work *more* on weekends, especially single-parent lawyers. I pour some leftover coffee into a mug, stick it in the microwave for thirty seconds, and drink it black while I stare at the business section of the paper. It beats the sports section, and I haven't looked at the full-color front page . . . well, since August.

My stomach growls. I open a cupboard and pull out a box of Toasty O's and one of our mismatched bowls. Half of them are gone, as are half our plates, half our silverware, half our glasses. Dad might as well have taken them all; Mom and I hardly eat at home anymore.

I grab the kitchen phone and dial his number to tell him off.

It rings twice—

"Hello . . . ?"

I yank the phone from my ear and hold it at arm's length, shocked that he *answered*—what was I going to say? In the milliseconds that pass, I hear him breathing, waiting . . .

"Cam? Buddy, are you there?"

I squeeze the receiver—I want to choke it.

I smash the phone into the cradle, stare at it, and repeat,

slamming plastic against plastic, over and over until a piece of it snaps off. I let go, and the receiver crashes to the floor and starts to beep that it's off the hook.

I lean against the counter and look at the shattered plastic on the floor.

My leg hurts.

If Viv were here, she'd make this all go away.

Or at least she'd know what to say.

I have to go back to the corner. Tonight. If there's any chance I'll see her again, this is it. I *saw* a ghost, there's no other explanation. And even though it wasn't Viv—there are lots of dead people—she has to be there too. Because if she isn't . . .

The universe just wouldn't *do* that to me.

FIVE

I STAND ON THE STREET CORNER BY THE SHRINE, AND THE STARS
are out.

Viv smiles at me from her pictures.

I walk halfway down the block and back, in both directions.
No one's here.

Nothing happens.

The air is finally starting to get that crisp, fall texture in addition to being cold. At least this time I have a jacket. I sit on a
rock and blow into my hands, itching for a cigarette. There's a
pack in my pocket, but I don't take it out. I guess I could look
for ghosts anywhere, but the only time I've seen one, I was here.
I wish I'd paid more attention to those ghost-hunting shows Viv
always wanted to watch. *We should be prepared, Cam,* she'd say.
What if someday we need to catch one? I swallow hard and try

to remember any episode where people actually made contact with the supernatural, but it seems like it was all lights turning on and off and crackly audio recordings. I don't remember any apparition showing up on camera and speaking.

But I know what I saw the other night. Why couldn't it have been *Viv*?

I stand up, pace, and peer around each side of the utility pole. Nothing.

I feel slightly pathetic, desperate, but somehow close to her.

And then a faint sound reaches my ears. I strain to listen. It's soft at first, but grows more distinct, as if it's getting closer. There's a grating quality to it, but the tone is unmistakably human. It sounds like someone . . .

Crying?

In three strides I've made it from the sidewalk, past the shrine, and into the bushes where it's louder, and I'm wondering if I should run again. There's a green glow behind the pole where there wasn't *anything* before.

Until the girl steps into view.

The light intensifies and it's impossible not to stare when she wipes a tear from her transparent cheek.

She studies me with the same haunted look as yesterday and holds my gaze a second too long. I have to glance away. The ghost girl wraps one arm around her waist and covers her mouth with the other, muffling a noise that seems to echo, like someone sobbing far away.

"Is there anyone else there with you?"

She looks confused. "What?"

"Is anyone *else* there?" My skin is cold and sweaty.

She fidgets uncomfortably. "Don't you recognize me?"

My mind races but comes up blank again and again. Her hair is long and smooth, though the color is simply a darker green than her skin. She's petite—with curves, but she's no Viv. I think I'd remember this girl's face, eyes huge and dark, but not weighed down with heavy makeup. She has a small, upturned nose and a pouty mouth that looks like it'd be cute if she smiled.

I've never seen this girl before in my life.

I shake my head.

Her eyes go flat; her hands fall to her sides.

I feel like I'm missing some huge puzzle piece. If she's a ghost, there should be some reason why I'm seeing her and not Viv.

Unless this is some kind of joke. . . .

The girl keeps fidgeting, rubbing something in her palm, and then I see what it is.

The lighter was a birthday present from Viv, and I *hate* how this strange girl is clutching it, like she owns some part of me. As if it belongs to her. Anger surges through my chest. I snatch at it before I can even consider *how* she might be holding it, and I watch my own hand *turn green* in front of me. My fingers brush hers—solid, warm—I pull back. My mouth is open. No sound comes out.

I hold my hand up. It looks normal again.

But it tingles where we touched.

She's staring at her hand too. I can see the green-tinted whites of her eyes, they're so wide.

I back away fast.

"Cam, wait!"

My heel hits a rock, and when my ass hits the ground my heart almost stops, but I'm on my feet in a second. I get to the middle of the empty blacktop, glance back, and stop.

She holds my silvery-green lighter in the palm of her outstretched hand, like she's offering it to me. This can't be happening—I'm *not* going back there. I don't want to go anywhere near this girl. But it's *my* lighter . . .

Viv gave it to me.

The girl's face is unreadable, and all I can think of are the Greek myths from humanities class last year, where men fall prey to monsters in female form. I'd think that's what would be happening to me now, if the monster had thought to appear as Viv.

She stretches her hand out farther. The Zippo looks big in her tiny palm, the metal eerily green. My initials are familiar in the neat, square script.

I swallow hard and walk toward her, hesitate, and reach into the light. Every nerve in my hand is tingling, but I grab the lighter, clutch it . . . and I can breathe. A fresh spring scent reaches me, like Viv's perfume, and I can almost feel the warm silk of her skin. I close my eyes.

"Cam, I've missed you. . . ."

Viv?

My skin tingles when we touch; I can tell she feels it too. It has to be her . . . isn't it? I don't want to open my eyes. I want to lay my lips on the soft skin beneath her wrist, trace up her arm to her mouth and melt into a never-ending kiss.

But she pulls me forward.

"Come back," she whispers.

I open my eyes and she *isn't* Viv. Two small, unfamiliar hands wrap around mine, and I can see through all three. The ghost girl is tugging me toward her, gently but firmly. My hand and arm up to my elbow are green. The strange translucence creeps up to my shoulder, across my chest, and it's like electricity under my skin. I look down, viewing my whole body green, and I think . . . I'm ready. I'll give myself up to whatever this is.

I'm about to close my eyes again when I glimpse Viv's face in a picture to my left. The colors are drab and earthy against the solid wooden pole—in contrast to the bright flash of green. Her expression seems to say, *Don't leave me.*

My eyes pop open. I pull back and dig my heels into the ground.

"No—" The girl falters, and I turn to see the panic in her eyes. I open my hand to shake her off, but she won't let go.

The monster's got me.

I shove her—as hard as I can. My hands connect with her shoulders, and she goes down. I haven't hit anyone that hard since football. For an excruciating moment, I don't think I'll make it back out of the green light. But I see the photos, I see Viv, and it's as if she guides me to safety. My body is buzzing all

32

over. I hang on to the pole, press my face into her picture when I'm safely out, praying for the energy to burn out of my skin. When it subsides enough that I'm no longer afraid to move, I sink to the ground. I crawl down the sidewalk until I'm far enough away, and throw up in the bushes.

SIX

IF I DON'T GET MY SHIT TOGETHER SOON, I'M SCREWED. I DECIDE
the best thing to do is act normal, pretend none of it ever
happened. I'll ask for extra hours at the grocery store in the
evenings so I don't have too much time alone; maybe I'll start
paying attention in class again—do homework. I've never seen
ghosts while surrounded by people at school . . . I rub at the skin
where she touched me, and shudder. Whatever that girl was, she
wasn't trying to help me find Viv.

If I try to explain what happened on the corner to Dr. Summers, she'll probably call it a "trauma trigger." She's mentioned it
before, that places associated with bad events can make people
crazy or something.

Only I *know* what I saw.

So I have until Friday at four o'clock—my next shrink

appointment—to get under control. Which means no more corner, and no transparent girls.

I walk between cars in the parking lot with my head up. Today is the first day all year I can't wait to get to school. People slam doors around me and I listen to them complain about the parties that got busted this weekend and the quizzes they have this week.

They sound so *normal.*

Monday-morning announcements drone on while I stare at my desk. Something about a fundraiser for the Model UN, exciting new items on sale at the school store, and a mandatory pep rally Friday afternoon. I've always wondered how they get away with calling it that—*mandatory.* Like they're going to make you go by holding a pom-pom to your head?

Everyone wear red and white for the team! Go Rams!

I see my shrink on Fridays for a reason.

I take a shortcut through a hallway that runs past the gym, trying to make it to trig on time for once. I avoid these particular halls when I can, and my leg gets me out of phys ed, but the familiar tile outside the locker rooms and the smells of sweat and weathered athletic equipment bombard my senses now. I get a burst of endorphins and have to remind myself that my playing days are over.

I'm holding my breath as I pass the locker-room doors, swinging and screaming on their hinges as kids filter in and out. I'm almost clear of them, ready to take a gulp of stale rest-of-the-school air when someone calls my name.

"Pike!"

I stop, letting my breath out through my teeth.

"Yeah, Co—Mr. Reed?"

"Can I see you a moment?"

"I'm going to be late for trig," I say.

"I'll write you a pass. It'll just take a minute."

He's gesturing to the nearby athletic office most of the coaches share, as opposed to his daytime, vice principal's digs. Not that it matters to me anymore. I step into the empty office.

Reed closes the door after me and stands behind the desk. He's wearing a gray suit and blue tie, which makes him look like he belongs in the coaches' office about as much as I do. Instinctively, my eyes wander everywhere else in the room. There's the shelf that's always been littered with mismatched, broken equipment. A box of brand-new uniforms sits open on the floor. Looks like girls' volleyball won the budget argument this year.

On the wall behind Reed is the trophy shelf. It's a little more crowded than last time I was in here, holding tall brass tributes to everything from swimming to basketball to golf, going back decades. My gaze is drawn to a huge framed photograph standing off to one side. I swallow hard, taking in the familiar red jerseys from freshman year, the first year we made States. I'd made junior varsity in middle school, but ninth grade was the year Andy Lowery hurt his shoulder in the first game. The other varsity quarterback had moved over the summer, so Logan and I were called up. He won some of his games—I won all of mine.

There's a tennis trophy in front of the photograph, but when I tilt my head to the side I can see, and I remember. Andy's standing at the back, holding my arm high. Logan's kneeling in the foreground, a familiar scowl on his face.

Blood roars through my ears. Reed gestures to the chair, and I sit down hard, trying to get my adrenaline in check. I feel like I'm about to run out on the field.

"How are things going, Cam?"

His voice brings me back into the room. I rub my right knee. "Fine."

He hesitates, sits down across from me. "Look, I know I'm not your coach anymore, but this has been a tough couple of months for all of us since Viv—since Miss Hayward . . ."

I clench my teeth. If *I* had died, would he be saying these same things to her?

"I'll be fine," I manage.

His forehead crinkles. "You've said that to me before."

I stare hard at the box of volleyball jerseys.

"I just can't help thinking about . . ." he continues, "after you broke your leg—"

"I was fine then, too," I say as evenly as possible. "Look, is this about what happened two months ago, or two years?"

He tugs at his tie where his whistle would hang at practice.

"It's about *you*. Today. Right now."

"And I told you, I'm *fine*."

"I bought that before, Camden. But your girlfriend isn't here to pick up the pieces for you this time."

I look up. "What is that supposed to mean?"

His face turns red.

"Is there a problem, Mr. Reed? I make it to classes; I turn in assignments; I'm not doing anything wrong."

I'm not doing much, but I should still graduate.

"No, you're right. Your grades are passable." Reed has been tapping a pen on the desk between his hands. He sets it down and sits back in his chair. "I only asked you in here because I'm worried. When you quit the team after your injury, you shut everyone out except Viv, but now—" He breaks off. No one ever wants to say *she's dead* out loud. "I just . . . don't want to see you give up like you did before."

I meet his gaze. "I appreciate the concern, Mr. Reed, but I *do* have a shrink." I rise from my chair. "Can I have that pass to trig?"

My heart pounds when I leave the office, but I ignore it, making a mental note never to come near the gym again. The boys' locker-room door swings open as I hurry past, almost hitting me in the face.

"Watch it," I say.

"No, *you* watch it, Pike." Logan shoves me into the wall. "Why the hell were you in there talking with Coach?"

My elbow throbs where it hit the tile. "What's it to you?"

We scowl at each other. I wait to see if he's going to kick my ass or not.

He speaks through his teeth. "I saw you with him the other day, too, out on the corner."

"So?"

"So—" He spits. "They'll never let you back on the team."

Back on the team?

"What the fuck are you talking about?"

He leans closer. "Everyone knows it's your fault she's dead."

Heat rolls from my head into my fists. I lunge at him, but he sees it coming. My shoulders hit the wall hard, pinned under Logan's palms. He holds me there, digging his fingers into my skin, with a look like he wants to crush my skull.

"If she'd stayed with me, she'd probably still be alive."

I glare at him, but we both know it's true.

He lets go abruptly and walks away down the hall.

When I get home, I throw my backpack on the couch. All I want to do is close the curtains and fall into bed . . . but I'm afraid to. Maybe the more tired I am, the less my brain will try to dream. I decide to call the grocery store and ask for an extra shift, but I wince when I see the broken phone on the counter by the fruit bowl, and the note that goes with it:

Cam—
Let's talk about this when I get home.
Love,
Mom

I flip the paper over and start to scrawl a response:

Mom—

Various excuses scroll through my mind:

The phone fell off the wall.
Don't worry; I smashed it because of Dad, not you.
Actually, if you were ever around, maybe he wouldn't have
left in the first place.

I throw the pen down, leaving the paper blank.

I glance at the clock. With any luck, I'll be the one at work when she gets home. I search my backpack for my cell to call the grocery store.

Except I have six missed calls from two numbers I don't recognize.

A knock sounds on the front door.

I flip the phone closed, straining to hear. It's probably a solicitor. Maybe the Mormons. I'm afraid of what I might say to someone preaching God today, so I creep toward the door and listen, waiting for them to go away.

The knock comes again. Louder.

"Shit."

God must have heard that, because whoever is outside starts pounding on the door.

I pull it open so fast I have to duck out of the way of a small fist.

My mouth drops open.

Staring up from my front step, her eyes brimming with tears, is the girl from the corner.

She isn't transparent. She isn't green.

She's real.

SEVEN

SHE SLUMPS AGAINST THE DOOR FRAME.

"Oh, thank God—you still live here." She wipes the back of her hand across her cheek. "I went to my house. Only it wasn't my house—"

She's here—on my doorstep. My stomach is empty, but I'm ready to heave. She straightens a little, presses her lips together, and looks at me expectantly. All I can do is stare.

She's a real, flesh-colored girl. Her jacket is gray; the skirt beneath it, dark blue. Her hair is a shiny, even shade of copper. Her eyes are brown, not green, and there are freckles on her nose. She isn't very tall.

"Do I *know* you?" I ask.

"Please, Cam, you've got to let me in."

I scan the street behind her, not sure what I'm looking for.

Someone hiding behind a bush, laughing? And then it hits me.

Logan.

"Who put you up to this?" I demand.

"No one—"

I ball up my fists. "Kind of a sick joke, don't you think?"

"Don't be crazy—"

My vision goes red. "It was Logan, wasn't it? I know it was Logan—"

"It's your fault I'm stuck here, *you* shoved me!"

I suck in a breath. She's touching her shoulder where I hit her last night.

"Look, I just want to get back home," she says.

There are dark circles under her eyes. Her hair is tangled, but she grips the door frame like she might rip it off to get in the house. I close my mouth and step aside. She comes in. I take one more suspicious look at the street. No reason to carry this on where they can watch . . . or record.

I close the door.

"What happened to this place?" she murmurs.

"What?"

"Nothing," she says quickly, but she doesn't tear her gaze from the room. She studies the furniture and shelves. I realize in this moment our two houseplants are dead.

She starts down the hall toward my room, like she's hypnotized or something, half floating, half stumbling. She doesn't even look at me, just passes by like I'm not even there. As if she knows exactly where to go. I start after her.

43

"Hey, you can't—"

She stops in the open doorway long enough to see in, and closes her eyes. I reach past her and bang the door shut. It echoes loudly down the hall and I'm glad for the noise because I'm ready to scream. I squeeze the doorknob.

"Everything's so wrong," she says. "Everywhere."

It's dim in the hall, and weird with both of us just standing here in front of my door. I loosen my grip on the knob.

"Who the hell *are* you?"

She doesn't say anything. She has to be working with Logan; there's no other answer. She's definitely not a ghost. I rub my forehead, exhausted, but she looks like she might pass out.

"Could I—" Her voice wavers. "Could I have a glass of water?"

The only ice in the freezer is crystallized on the outside of an old bag of peas. I fill a glass with cold water at the sink and set it down in front of her.

"Thanks," she says, sliding onto a stool at the breakfast bar.

I wonder what school she goes to, how he knows her. I wait until she's gulped down half the glass before saying anything. She sets it on the counter. Her eyes are calm now, her pupils not quite so large. She's probably rehearsed this.

"You feel better?" I ask.

She doesn't answer, but she looks miserable. Nice touch. I lean against the wall where the phone used to go. She won't look me in the eye—she can't be that good. She starts to ask something, and stops.

"What?" I ask.

She shakes her head.

"What were you going to say?"

She presses her lips together, and I study her while she studies the floor. I wonder how Logan pulled off making her appear transparent. Or did my own mind provide that extrasensory detail? I clench my jaw. Her hands are clearly opaque now. They don't pass through the water glass, but every time she moves, I still expect her to start glowing or something.

I shake it off.

"So, did he offer to pay you for this?"

"I told you, this isn't a joke." She closes her eyes. "I wish it were."

I snort. "What, you're really a ghost?"

"*I'm* not the ghost," she chokes.

"Then what are you?"

"I'm alive." She bites her lower lip, considering. "But I think I'm in the wrong place."

I fold my arms across my chest. "And that's somehow my fault?"

"Yes."

She shifts stiffly, as if she's uncomfortable, and I remember how hard I shoved her. I realize just how sore and bruised she probably is, and that *is* my fault. The back of my neck gets hot. But I thought she was a ghost!

"What did you mean . . . in the wrong place?" I ask.

She pushes her hair out of her face with an unsteady hand. "I didn't notice anything different at first. It took forever just to catch my breath and climb out of the bushes after you pushed me." She glances at me and swallows. "But when I tried to go home last night, some other family was living in my house . . . and that's not the only thing. Granted, it was two in the morning, but I went to my friend's house, and her dad *chased* me out of the yard—I've known Mr. Caccione since I was ten!" Her voice rises. "I spent the night drinking coffee at McDonald's, calling everyone I could think of from the pay phone, but they all hung up on me or didn't answer." She picks up the empty glass and stares into it. "When I tried the school this morning, the front office had never heard of me either . . . so when I saw you, I followed you home. Only this is all wrong too!"

The glass slips from her fingers and shatters spectacularly all over the floor.

"Oh! I'm sorry!"

I watch a fragment spin across the tile and skid to a stop against the wall. She's off her stool, trying to pick up the shards. I move to touch her shoulder, but stop myself. I don't want to play into her.

"I'll get it later."

She looks at my hand still hovering over her, and flinches away. She backs up, sits on the barstool, and hugs herself.

"Either everyone's playing a cruel joke on me, or—"

"A cruel joke on *you*?" I say.

She shakes her head, tears streaming down her cheeks. "It's just . . . like I don't exist."

This girl could win an Oscar.

"Yeah, well, I've never seen you before."

She smacks her hand down on the table.

46

"My name is Nina Larson! I go to Fowler High School! I live at Twenty-six Genesee Street with my idiot aunt and little brother, who *needs* me!" Her voice breaks and she covers her face with her hands. "You have to help me, Cam."

My skin prickles when she says my name.

I rest my head in my hand, and fight with myself. Don't indulge the joke, don't play along. I would have made sure she was okay if I'd seen her hurt in the bushes last night—if I knew she was even real. But she's an actress and she's trying to make me feel bad . . . I take in the face and the tears. He probably hired her just for her tragic looks. Or maybe—

Maybe Logan is fucking with her, too?

No, that's too much, even for him. She has to be in on it. I should test her; see if I can poke a hole in her story. I rack my brain for every weird sci-fi book, story, movie, or TV show I've ever seen. I remember one show about strange encounters where a hunter said he was in the woods when a man appeared out of thin air, walking through the trees, and disappeared again. He'd been dressed in a uniform from the Revolutionary War.

"What's the date where you're from?" I ask gamely.

She points at today's newspaper spread over the counter. "Same as today. I thought of that. I'm *not* a time traveler." She focuses intently on the paper in front of her, and then steals a glance at me. "But I think I know . . . how to get back."

"Then why don't you do it?"

She tears at the edge of the paper, turning the margin into neat shreds.

"I tried. I went back to the corner during the day today. I thought—since that's where it happened before—maybe there's a way back. But I couldn't find anything."

And there it is. "So, Logan sent you to lure me back to the corner. What's he got planned? Has he invited the whole school to come out and laugh at me—call me crazy? Make sure I don't try to get back on the team?"

She looks me straight in the eye. "My skin tingled when we touched last night."

Whatever words I was going to say next die on my lips. I curl one hand into a fist, the same hand she grabbed yesterday. I can almost feel the electric sensation still dancing under my skin. How could Logan have orchestrated *that*?

"You felt it too?"

She grimaces and nods. "It made me think . . . maybe I need *you* to get back."

"No."

"You pushed me . . ."

"No way."

"And I ended up here—"

"I can't—"

She slips off her stool and comes right up to me, desperate. "Maybe if we try the same thing again, I'll go back!"

I jerk away from her. "I'm not going back there with you!"

I rub my eyes and stare at her, looking like a frightened animal, yet sitting in my kitchen like the very fact she's here is nothing new. Logan can't make me look dumb if I know what he's up to . . . but something nags at me deep down.

A tingling under my skin.

When we reach Fowler High School, it's obvious we'll have to wait until dusk. The weather is chilly but clear, and the campus is crawling with activity. The track team runs laps around the block, jogging past Viv's shrine, again and again. A group of skaters do ollies in the parking lot. I don't look at the athletic field.

Since I'm exhausted, and ghost girl looks like she's ready to claw her way back wherever she came from, I buy us each a cup of coffee at the gas station down the block. I lean against the bus shelter. She sits. Neither of us says much. I can't help looking at her. Her cheeks are pink with cold, which looks kind of odd against the color of her hair. Not striking, the way Viv's looked with her dark eyes and curls, but pretty enough in her own way. I turn my Zippo over in my fingers, think about lighting a cigarette, but I don't. A bus pulls up, the door opens. When neither of us moves, the driver gives us a look that probably sums up his Monday, and drives on.

"That means a lot to you?" she asks.

I follow her gaze to the lighter in my hand.

"You just keep staring at it," she says. "But you don't smoke."

"I thought I lost it," I mutter.

"When I came to the corner the other morning, it just came clattering out of the bushes." Her voice brightens. "I would never have seen you if I hadn't looked to find out where it came from."

I roll my eyes and put the Zippo back in my pocket. I'm done listening to her stories.

She looks at her lap.

By the time everyone has either driven away or had their parents come get them, it's gotten dark. We walk across the street side by side, and I'm startled by the headlights of a slow-moving car. The beams slide over both of us. She squints, and moves closer to me. I try not to jerk away. The street gets dark again. The corner of campus seems deserted compared to half an hour ago, though I'm secretly relieved. If this still turns out to be a setup, there won't be many witnesses.

We pass the shrine. Viv's pictures, the notes, the stuffed animals. She slows when we get to the pole, lingering on the images.

"What?" I ask.

"Nothing, I just—" She shakes her head. "I used to know her."

"*You* knew Viv?" I stop and clamp my mouth shut. Is this part of the act too? Would she dare take it that far? Or if it's the truth . . . how did they know each other? I knew everything about Viv. How could I have missed that?

She looks more closely at the notes. "It was a car accident?"

I can't unlock my jaw. My teeth are too tightly clenched. I manage to nod my head, but I think it looks more like a shudder.

"I'm sorry," she whispers, looking away.

We're standing under the street light, which is just flickering on. It's dark at the base of the pole and in the bushes. No eerie green lights anywhere.

"Now what?" I say through my teeth, glancing around for

Logan. I just want to get this whole fucking thing over with.

She takes a deep breath, steps into the bushes, and starts moving around, waving her arms randomly. It stays dark, and she stays here. If she isn't an actress, maybe *she's* crazy. I wonder if she'd like to meet Dr. Summers. She steps back out of the shrubs.

"Still doesn't work." She glances around as if looking for something she missed. Then she swallows hard and stammers. "I—I guess maybe we should try holding hands?"

Oh, hell no. I shove my hands in my pockets and stare at her, but she's serious. She bites her lip and holds out one hand. My leg aches. I shift from my right foot to my left. I didn't think this could get any weirder. But if it helps me get rid of her . . .

"Okay."

She approaches slowly, and I hold out my right hand so she doesn't get any closer. She takes it with her left. Her touch is gentle, warm, but not the least bit tingly.

I wonder, for the first time, what *will* happen next? Will Logan leap out of the bushes, then post a video of this online? Will she turn back into a ghost and disappear?

She tugs me forward, and I have this horrible déjà vu about being pulled into that green light, only it stays dark. We trample through the bushes, making a wide circuit around the utility pole. I take secret joy in kicking the prickly shrubs. This feels like some bizarre game of ring-around-the-rosy.

After several minutes of this, she starts jerking my wrist, like if she yanks hard enough, she can somehow *make* something happen. I catch her eye, and her face contorts. She looks away, but fresh tears shine on her cheeks in the faint street light.

"Um, maybe we should get closer to the pole," I mumble. "It seems like . . . it was closer before . . . I don't know."

She just nods, and I pull her along this time, feeling ridiculous. I glance at Viv's pictures looking back at me, and I feel totally wrong holding this strange girl's hand. I hope Viv knows that she's the only one *ever*. I hope she understands.

We stop against the front of the pole. Nothing has changed. My hand is getting stiff from being squeezed, but I don't say anything. Ghost girl's looking around like she wants to tear the place apart, and I almost tell her it's okay—that happens to me too. But then she lets go of my hand and flips her hair over her shoulder.

The ends of it glow green.

It's just for a second, and when the strands fall back down around her shoulders, they look normal. I don't trust myself to blink, so I reach past her with my free hand, right behind the pole where I saw it happen, and watch my fingertips turn green.

They tingle. Is this . . . real?

"Here," I gasp.

She turns around and sucks in a breath. She reaches below where I hold my hand, where the air looks dark and normal, and sinks her fingertips in too. Her nails start to glow, and she pushes in to her knuckles, and then she's up to her wrist in green. I watch with my mouth open. I can barely breathe. She lets go of my other hand, and starts walking into the light, but I grab her sleeve.

"Wait—are you sure about this?"

She turns to me, face pained. "I can't stay here. I have to get home—my brother."

Half her body appears normal, but the other half has gone transparent and glowing. I blink and widen my eyes. Seeing through her the first time was one thing, but watching her step in, *become* transparent . . .

I point into the light. "What if that doesn't take you home?"

She leans all the way in, so far that half of her disappears completely and her lower half is all green. I'm relieved when she straightens, entirely transparent, but otherwise in one piece.

"This looks like home . . . but I guess it does there, too," she says uncertainly.

Her voice has that metallic quality, like the first time I saw her, only now the tone is softer. Her eyes have turned back from brown to green, but they're filled with resolve.

She forces a smile. "It was great to see you again, Cam."

I open my mouth, not sure what to say. She can't just leave—she never said how she knows me, *or* Viv. Where's she from? Where does the light go? How is any of this even possible? My mind races with things I would've asked if I'd just believed her sooner.

But before I can say anything, she turns away again, quickly, and vanishes with the light.

I wait a couple of long minutes. It's quiet out here, alone in front of the school, too cold for crickets. A dog barks somewhere in the neighborhood. A siren wails faintly, rising and falling in the distance. Nothing happens by the wooden pole. I'm afraid to move.

Where did she go?

My breaths are short. I lift my hand, and I'm about to touch my fingers to the empty air again, but I stop. What if I reach out and the green light is still there? What if it isn't? A gust of wind sweeps through my hair, sending a chill into my skin. I pull my hand back and my jacket closer.

Do I just leave now? I stare into the night air, afraid to look away or turn my back on the pole. I half hope for something else to happen, half pray it won't. Even if something else *did* happen, I'm not sure I trust my eyes anymore. Did I really see a girl here? Did she walk out of thin air and spend the afternoon at my house? I kick a rock into the street, listening to it bounce solidly across the asphalt. My lips curl back from my teeth and I laugh out loud, but my voice breaks and I clap one hand over my mouth to stop the sound.

I touch the utility pole carefully, running my fingers over the cards and pictures that connect me to Viv. I reach for the nearest one—the cheerleading shot—and tear it down, but I hesitate once it's in my hand. The empty spot where it used to hang looks wrong, like something's missing. I start to panic, try to put it back in place, but the staples and tape don't cooperate. After several minutes, I give up. The paper is wrinkled, so I smooth it out until Viv's smile looks almost right, and tuck it in my pocket. You'd never know what happened to her without this shrine. I glance warily at the spot where the ghost girl—Nina—disappeared. I could be mistaken, but I swear it's the *same* spot.

Two girls have disappeared here. And I'm still alone, without even a ghost.

EIGHT

I FUMBLE WITH MY HOUSE KEY. IT'S DARK INSIDE, BUT MOM'S CAR is in the driveway, so I tiptoe in and lock up as quietly as I can. I spent the evening outside a gas station sipping coffee after coffee, gripping the Styrofoam cup tight in my hands. I feel like I need to touch everything I see, just to make sure it won't disappear. My head is foggy, and despite the caffeine, I don't feel any more awake than I did this morning. This night is already starting to seem like a weird dream, and right now, I'm okay believing that's exactly what it was.

I have to pass through the living room to make it to my bedroom. Mom is asleep on the couch, bathed in the light of the TV. The sound of an old sitcom laugh track whispers through the air. She's still in her work clothes, shoes on the floor. Nothing unusual. She sleeps out here now more than in the bedroom she shared with Dad.

I feel the promising pull of my own bed down the hall, but I hesitate by the couch. She looks so small, curled into a ball like that. I decide to get her a blanket from the linen closet, but before I can take another step, she speaks.

"Late night, Cammer?"

"Didn't think you were awake . . . it's not that late."

She sits up and stretches, holding her watch in the blue light of the TV. "Guess it isn't."

Laughter titters from the speakers. Mom hits the mute button and pats the cushion next to her.

"I was kinda hoping to get to bed," I say, walking around the coffee table to sit beside her. "Trig quiz tomorrow."

"How's school going?"

"Fine."

She twists her fingers together in her lap.

"Your dad called again today. He said he's been trying to email you too—"

"I don't care."

I stare at happy black-and-white families moving silently on the screen.

"Cam, Dr. Summers called. She was concerned about you."

"Oh . . ." The broken kitchen telephone pushes its way into my exhausted mind. I rub my eyes. "Sorry about the phone. I'll buy a new one."

"You want to tell me why there was glass all over the kitchen floor too?"

"What?"

Then I remember. I give myself a head rush, I stand up so fast. I flip the light on in the kitchen. The tile floor is bare, but the dustpan is on the counter, full of glass and dirt.

"I swept it up . . . thankfully before I cut myself wide open," Mom says, coming up behind me and squeezing my shoulder. "Sweetie, what's going on?"

I brace myself in the doorway. The kitchen counter is spread with newspaper, one side of which has been torn into neat shreds. Two barstools are positioned like people were sitting there together. Me. And her.

It really happened.

I shrug Mom's hand off my shoulder, and suppress a shiver.

"Nothing, I just—forgot, sorry."

"Cam—"

"How was court today?" I ask. "You kick some prosecutor ass?"

"Honey . . ." She takes off her glasses. "I told Dr. Summers that maybe we should think about medication."

I close my eyes, only because I know she isn't looking at my face. Happy pills—so you don't have to feel. They've tried to get me on them before. I don't want to live without Viv, but the pain of missing her is better than no feeling at all.

"No."

"We don't have to decide tonight, I just mentioned—"

"*No*, Mom."

She doesn't think I've noticed that she stepped farther away, that her voice has gotten small. She's waiting to see what comes after a broken telephone and shattered glass, and there was a time I might have broken a few more things.

"I don't need it," I say calmly.

Then she surprises me; she takes my hand and looks up into my face. She used to have this helmet hair before Dad left. I don't know if she hasn't bothered to cut it or what, but I think she looks younger the way she does it now, piled brownish-gray on top of her head. Without her glasses, all the hazel colors in her eyes stand out. She seems shorter, but then I remember her heels lying on the floor.

"I'm proud of how you've been dealing with—everything." Her voice quavers. She won't say Viv's name. She never does. "But you have to promise me you won't miss any more appointments with your doctor. You *need* her right now."

"Okay . . . I promise."

Mom gives my arm a little squeeze, tips up on her toes, and pecks me on the cheek. I give her a weak hug, mumble something about trigonometry, go to my room, and slump against the closed door.

I am sitting in Dr. Summers's waiting/living room, but it's only Tuesday morning. Lance pants loudly at my feet. This was the only appointment open before Friday, which is fine because I want to get this out of the way sooner rather than later. So much for getting my shit together. I don't know what I'm going to have to say to stay off meds, but I'm not leaving with a prescription, even if she thinks I *am* crazy. I place my hands on my knees and stare at my knuckles. Finally, the door opens and Dr. Summers emerges to see her first patient out.

Lance whines when we enter the office and close the door behind us. Dr. Summers heads for her chair with a cup of coffee, as she often does. She has on one of her plethora of beige sweaters. The dog is outside the door. The clock ticks rhythmically on the wall. All of this makes me relax. Nothing too weird—except this isn't Friday.

"I know my mom talked to you," I say before she's totally settled. She takes an extra second to cross her legs.

"And I know what she probably said," I continue. "So I just came in to let you know I've given it some thought, but I'm not going on any meds."

She waits a long time before speaking, letting the silence creep under my skin.

"So how come you think your mom wants you to?"

"She told me. I was standing right in front of her—"

"No, I meant what do you think *caused* her to feel that way?"

I shift on the couch and stare at the wheels of her chair.

"I don't know."

"Is there a reason she might be more worried about you lately?"

There are a zillion reasons my mom should be worried about me lately—*I'm* worried about me—but I'm not sitting here for any of those reasons. I'm here to avoid the pharmacy, not get a ride over there. But that's exactly where I'll be if I tell Dr. Summers about the strange girl I met yesterday who said she *used to know Viv*, then disappeared into thin air.

I need a diversion.

"It's dumb," I say. "No big deal. I was upset at Dad. . . . A couple things in the kitchen got broken."

She raises an eyebrow. "It's been a while since you've gotten angry like that."

Ugh—bad plan. I grit my teeth. Part of what made them want to put me on meds in the first place was anger. Before Viv made me realize none of it—none of them—was worth the rage. She'd stay so calm when I got mad, I could never manage to stay upset. As long as we had each other, nothing else mattered. My chest aches. I really don't want to drag her into this, especially since she had nothing to do with the broken phone or the shattered glass, but she's the one thing nobody will question.

"I was just . . . missing Viv."

Dr. Summers's face is maddeningly sympathetic.

"It's just, I never felt like I needed to talk to Dad before she—" I stop. Take a breath. "So I tried calling him."

"How'd that go, Cam?"

I open my mouth and close it, glancing at the clock while I try to decide what to say, and, more important, what not to say.

"Not so good," I say, hoping she'll fill in the blanks how she wants.

"Oh?"

I look up, wanting this to be a rhetorical *Oh?* But all I get is an expressionless shrink-stare. I press one hand to my temple and close my eyes, trying not to think how Dad's been the one calling and sending email, and I've been ignoring it. How when he answered the phone, I was madder at myself than at him— because he might've thought I missed him.

"I'm just not ready to really talk to him, okay?"

Dr. Summers gives me one of her assessing stares. The kind robots scan people with in sci-fi movies before either shooting them or letting them go. "We can come back to this. But I'm glad you called him when you were upset."

I unfold my hands, palms sweaty, glance at the clock, and laugh a little too loudly. "Things could be worse. It's not like I'm talking to little green men or anything..."

She raises her eyebrows. "I hope you would tell me if you started seeing little green men, Cam."

I rub the back of my neck. How about little green *girls*?

"I'll let you know if it ever happens," I say quickly, and wonder again if she sees straight through my lies. "But seriously, getting upset with my dad for not being around when my life sucks? Not worth a prescription, in my personal opinion."

"I agree."

"Really?"

She nods, setting her mug aside. "I'm not suggesting there won't be a time to reconsider that option, but you've proven me wrong before. I didn't think you'd make it without meds initially, but you had been doing remarkably well this past year..."

She leaves the last part unsaid: *until Viv died.*

The snail-like minute hand on the wall clock inches forward.

I stay drug free if I just keep saying the right things.

I surprise myself with a truth.

"I want to keep doing well without them—for Viv."

Dr. Summers smiles. "I think that's reasonable."

NINE

"WHAT'S UP?" MIKE ASKS. THE BASS COMING FROM HIS EARBUDS is cranked so high I know exactly which obnoxious indie rock song is playing before he shuts the music off.

"Hey," I say, closing *Ethan Frome*. I thought I'd try reading our English assignment during lunch instead of just staring at the pages while everyone else eats, but the characters are getting to me, and my mind keeps wandering. I walked past Viv's memorial on the way to school, but it didn't look any different. I didn't hear Nina's voice. I stare into space and wonder why her green-light-portal thing came through *there*. I wish for the hundredth time that I had asked Nina how she knew Viv.

Mike interrupts my thoughts. "So the whole team is gonna grab something to eat at Fast Break after practice . . ."

"Um, have fun."

I start thumbing through my book, looking for the page I'd been staring at.

He clears his throat. "I was kind of thinking maybe you'd come too."

I stop turning pages, but I don't look up.

"I'm not on the team anymore."

"You don't have to be on the team just to come hang out."

I snap the book shut and stuff it into my bag. Fast Break is the dingy late-night diner we sometimes went to after practices, and after every game. The guys would sit on one side of the room and the cheerleaders on the other. I bite my lip at the memory. Freshman year, before Andy Lowery got hurt and I got bumped up to starting quarterback, I was sitting in the sticky booths surrounded by other Fowler Rams when I got my first glimpse of Viv. We'd just finished practice and I felt amazing. When the cheerleaders came in, the guys started whistling and calling, so I joined in. The older girls ignored us, but when Viv turned, glowing and smiling from her very first practice, I stopped. She walked to the adjacent booth and sat in Logan's lap. My heart sank when he put a possessive arm around her, but then she looked up and our eyes met.

I winked. Viv smiled. Logan never saw it coming.

It seems like another life.

Mike is looking at me like he thinks I've actually stepped inside Fast Break in the last two years. Like going there now would be no big deal. I glance down the hall toward the cafeteria. A group of people loiters outside the door, and I spot Logan among them.

He pinches Tash Clemons's ass. The cheerleader whips around shrieking, feigning anger and failing at flirtation.

"Thanks . . . I just can't," I say.

Mike follows my gaze and grunts. "Come on, West's a dick, but everyone else—"

I shake my head. I won't win any favors with everyone else at this point.

He furrows his brow and wads up his energy-bar wrapper.

"The new place then, Dina's Diner? Across the street."

"What?"

He sighs. "We used to hang out all the time, Cam."

He's right. Even after my injury, when Viv turned in her pom-poms and I didn't return to practice, he invited us out—both of us. The cheer squad turned catty, the team stopped talking to me, but Mike never bought the bullshit. It's not like he quit football in support or anything, he just kept treating me and Viv the way he did everyone. So when Viv suggested we avoid him to spare his reputation, I couldn't really argue. *He's an adorable, loyal puppy,* she'd said. *No one wants to hurt a puppy.*

I glance at the open notebook in his lap. Today he's sketching some kind of hairy monster—he's always drawing monsters or girls. Grabbing food with Mike would be a normal thing to do. And I might actually be spending time with someone who wants my company. These days my doctor and my mom are the only people happy to see me, and one of them gets paid by the other for the privilege.

"Um, okay, I guess—"

"Hey, man, I'm not asking you on a date," he says.

I can't help it; I laugh. "You think this new place has chili fries anything like Fast Break?"

"The ones that burn all the way down? I doubt it." Mike pops me in the shoulder. "Fry judgment—six o'clock. See you there."

The air is frosty and still as I cross the parking lot of Dina's Delicious Diner—*Now Open!* It hasn't snowed yet, but the clear sky seems eager to pull a blanket of clouds over itself.

I glance at the half-burned-out orange neon sign across the street. It says FAST over the door, and I guess no one can argue with that. The garage-door walls and rusted light fixtures angled over the parking lot suggest Fast Break used to be a run-down gas station. Now it looks like a run-down gas station someone converted into a restaurant. It's even dingier than I remember, or maybe it's just decayed two more years since I bothered to notice. People I used to know are crammed into hard blue plastic booths by the windows, huddled over chili fries and giant chocolate shakes. It would be easy to cross the street, open the door, and walk in.

It's easier not to.

I pull open Dina's door and am met with green carpet, warm wooden furniture, and chickens . . . everywhere. They're painted all over the hostess stand, decorate the curtains, and are perched on high shelves, leering at me behind waxy plastic plants. There's a display case in the foyer with at least twelve different kinds of pie, all guarded by colorful ceramic and stuffed fowl. The place is busy, but I spot Mike waiting in a booth across the room.

I weave my way behind a table of saggy old men, and around a mother trying to herd two little kids to the bathroom. I sink into the cushy green seat across from Mike and find myself eye to eye with what looks like an actual rooster . . . or what used to be. I slide it down the table toward the window.

"What's with the chickens?" I ask.

Mike opens his mouth, but our waitress comes, so he shakes his head and stifles a laugh. I get my answer when she hands us each a menu, and I acquaint myself with Dina's Delicious assortment of Country Burgers, Country Steaks, Country Potatoes, Country Gravy, and Country Pies. Apparently if you want to eat country food, it is best done in the ambiance of a quaint barnyard.

"I kind of doubt they serve Country Chili Fries," Mike whispers.

They don't, but we order something called Country Poutine, which is supposed to consist of french fries, country gravy, and cheese curd. Close enough.

I fidget while we wait for our food. The chickens seem to be staring at me from all over the room. Viv would've hated them too.

"Hey, isn't that—" Mike stops. "I think I recognize that girl."

I swivel in my seat, but the room is full of families and I can't tell who he's pointing at.

"Who?"

"That girl, over there?" He snaps his fingers, then points at me and grins. "Isn't she the girl I saw you with last night?"

I inhale soda, and it drips into my lungs and out my nose. I cough until the room looks like a blur of green and gold feathers through my carbonation-stung eyes. I try to focus, and think I see a copper-colored head, but it ducks into the kitchen before my vision clears.

"I wasn't with a"—I cough again and take in a ragged breath—"girl last night."

Mike looks at me funny. "I drove right by you on the corner after practice. I was going to stop, but the way you both looked . . . I thought she might be a relative of Viv's or something." He gestures across the room. "Do you want to say hi?"

I look up, and forget how to breathe all over again. *Nina* is standing on the other side of the room taking an order. She's wearing a green apron with her hair pulled back. There's a pen tucked behind her ear and she's smiling . . . but it's her.

She's here.

The noise in the restaurant rises to a clamor inside my head. The room is too warm, too small. The fluorescents are too bright. The chickens stare glassy-eyed from every corner. This is worse than opening my door and finding her on my porch, because Mike's here watching—he's pointing her *out*. I can't believe he's part of it. I'm the biggest idiot in town.

"Did Logan put you up to this?" I demand. "Is this a fucking joke?"

"Logan? Wait, what?"

"Tell me." I slam my fist on the table. "Because I never thought you—"

"Whoa." He holds up his hands. "What are you talking about, Cam?"

It doesn't make sense. *I saw her disappear.* Logan couldn't have orchestrated that. But if she went back to wherever she came from, why is she taking a dinner order across the room?

I watch Nina laughing with the patrons, a light pink blush coloring her cheeks. She hasn't seen me. She goes behind the register alone, and I'm out of my seat, making my way through the barnyard. I get to the counter and lean over, unblinking, so I won't miss her expression when she does notice me.

She looks up with a smile, catches my eye, and says, "How was dinner tonight?"

"What?"

"Did you get to try a slice of our Country Pecan Pie?"

The freckles on her nose bunch up when she smiles. I check her name tag, uncertain.

HELLO, MY NAME IS: NINA

"That's all you have to say?"

Her smile wavers.

"I'm sorry, was there a problem with your meal, sir?"

"*Sir?*"

I start to reach for her, but Mike appears next to me and grips my arm like a vice. I try to wrench him off me, but he holds fast. He throws money down on the counter.

"Here, sorry, we thought you were someone else. . . . Sorry."

She looks from me to Mike to the money, and back to me. Her brown eyes go from confusion to concern, but never hint at recognition as Mike hauls me out the door.

When we're in the parking lot, he lets go and puts some distance between us.

"What the hell was that?" he demands.

I can't speak, but out here, I can breathe again. I squat and rest my head in my hands, trying to make sense of—everything. That she was there, not gone . . .

"Cam?" Mike asks uneasily.

One thought keeps playing over in my mind, but I know I'm wrong. I *saw* her disappear.

"Logan West is fucking with me!"

"Logan?" Mike asks, bewildered. "What did *that* have to do with Logan?"

I stand up and stare at Fast Break across the street.

"He has to be paying that girl. She's in on it too."

"I don't think—" Mike hesitates, but when he speaks again, his voice is level. "Maybe—maybe I shouldn't have pushed you to come out tonight. . . ."

I roll my eyes and walk across the dark, empty street. Logan is going to pay.

"Cam? Where are you going?" He runs to catch up.

My jaw tightens against the cold. All I can see are the lit-up garage-door windows in front of me. Logan's inside, at the center of the group. Tash is squished in next to him, giggling and running her hand through his hair. The girls all look like they want to throw her under a bus. Logan sits there like he's the master of the universe. I used to look just like him, and it makes me want to puke.

Mike's firm grip stops me for the second time tonight, and I'm reminded of how much better shape he's in than me. I jerk away.

"You don't want to do this," he says.

I grab the door handle, and suddenly, this isn't just about tonight. "I've wanted to do this for two years."

"Okay, fine, then." Mike speaks so fast, he almost trips over his words. "But do yourself a favor, don't do it in front of them." He jerks his thumb over one shoulder. "He won't need to lift a finger. You'll never have a chance."

I hesitate, taking in the size of the crowd gathered around Logan. Ten? Fifteen people?

"Let me go get him," Mike says. "I'll bring him out here to you."

I spit. "No way."

"What do you think *Viv* would tell me to do, Cam? Stand here and watch you get slaughtered?"

My chest aches. I speak through my teeth. "You have two minutes."

He opens the door and doesn't look back.

I don't watch him approach Logan. I turn the corner where I can't be seen and stare through another window. There's a guy and a girl at a booth in the far corner. I can't make out their faces. They're huddled close, smiling at each other, insulated against the post-practice chaos carrying on around them.

Logan shoves out the door, tugging Tash behind him like a toy. Mike follows. A few people point out the windows, but no one else joins in.

"You have something to say to me, Pike?"

He stands with his feet apart, arms at his sides. Nonconfrontational.

I meet his gaze, and his eyes are clear, but then I see it . . . a slow smirk creeping up from the edge of his mouth. This is all a fucking game to him.

I launch my fists at him. Tash screams, but before I can get a punch in, Mike's hands are on my shoulders, pulling me away.

"If you want to fuck with me, do it to my face!" I yell.

Logan stands his ground, though I missed his nose by inches. The smirk is gone, but he looks more annoyed than anything. I elbow Mike in the gut, and he lets go, coughing to catch his breath.

"Just leave me the hell alone!"

Logan brushes at his sleeve, no worse off for my knuckles never reaching his face.

"Look, Pike, I don't have time for this," he says, sounding bored. "Get some help." He snakes his arm around Tash's waist, and turns to go back inside.

"You're paying that girl—" My voice breaks. "To try and convince me I'm crazy!"

Logan stops and exchanges a look with Mike. He turns his gaze back to me.

"Pike . . . really, do you need convincing?"

TEN

EVERYONE THINKS I'VE LOST IT.

I sit on the curb behind Fast Break, staring at a cigarette butt and a flattened bottle cap at my feet. The parking lot smells faintly of gasoline. I pick at my fingernail. Mike left an hour or so ago, telling me to call him. Around midnight the restaurant empties—it's a school night, after all. Someone trips over me taking a bag of trash to the Dumpster. I don't move. I sit long after the neon lights go out behind me.

I should go home.

I pull myself up and aim in that direction. My bed waits there, ready to transport me to tomorrow, and the next day, and the next. I put one foot in front of the other. But by the time I get moving, I'm not headed for my house anymore.

When I reach the utility pole, I'm gasping for air. I don't

remember when I started running, but after I got going I couldn't slow down, even when my leg began to ache.

There's got to be something here—some proof it *happened*. I'm not crazy.

I lean against the dark wood to keep from collapsing. One of Viv's remembrance cards flutters to the sidewalk. When I can breathe without my lungs feeling like they're on fire, I study the shrine. Dead petals litter the ground; I should have brought more flowers last week. There's a big blank spot where a picture of Viv is missing. My heart seizes up until I remember, and I pull the wrinkled cheerleading photo from my pocket.

I stare at her face a long time and circle the pole, comparing the wide-eyed grin of freshman year to her more mature expressions in later pictures. The most recent was my own addition. I almost didn't put it up, but I didn't want her shrine constructed entirely by *them*. The shot was taken on a camping trip a week before her death. We were out in the woods, in the middle of nowhere. We climbed up a rocky ledge to watch the sunset. I called her name and took the picture before she saw what I was doing. Her expression is questioning, her eyes dark and content. Behind her, a brilliant orange and gold sky blazes over the treetops, marking the end of the day, the end of summer. On that trip we felt like the only two people left on earth. She kissed me and said, *I've never been so happy.*

I give the shrubs a halfhearted kick. The memorial looks like it always does. I'm not sure what I expected to find. The streetlight above me flickers but stays dim. I look over my shoulder, afraid

Nina will show up with Logan this time, still wearing her apron from Dina's Delicious Diner. They'll come to laugh with Tash and Mike while I flail in the bushes, searching for my sanity.

What if Logan really *is* making me crazy?

I ball my hand into a fist, but there's nothing to hit, so I take a swing at the shadow of the pole, where it used to stand, at the exact place where I imagine Viv's head hit the glass.

There's a flash of green, and my knuckles tingle.

I stare into the darkness.

There's nothing there.

I reach out . . . my fingers glow transparent green. I'm not imagining this. It's like penetrating the surface of water so clear you can't see it until your fingers are swimming, and just by touching it you're aware its depths are something foreign and unexplored. I repeat this routine three or four more times, then reach my arm all the way in and leave it there. The electrical sensation pulses under my skin, all the way to my bicep. It isn't what I'd call comfortable, but it doesn't hurt.

I'm not crazy—I can *see* this. I glance around, looking for the source of the freaky green glow, but when I put my hands down, it disappears. I reach back out, more comfortable when the light is clearly in front of me—when I can't question its existence. I wish I could figure out what it *was*. I wave my arm around, and it bumps into something. I'm clearly hitting the utility pole to my left, but to the right my arm seems to be stopped by empty air. I reach forward, and don't feel anything but tingly space. I can still see the school straight ahead, through the green. I hold my breath and take a step, stick my face into the light. My nose and cheeks buzz with energy, and when I open my eyes and look at my hands, they're see-through. I can *see through* my skin, veins, bone—I'm getting nauseous. This isn't real—

This is real.

I start to pull back to safety, but when I gaze ahead through the green, something about the facade of the school makes me stop. It looks different. I narrow my eyes, but my whole head tingles now; it's hard to concentrate. Something Nina said when I saw her disappear echoes faintly in my mind: *This looks like home . . . but I guess it does there, too.*

I blink, take a step forward, and then I realize what it is. The art-room window. It should be boarded up from a kiln fire—it has been for nearly a year. I know, because Viv and I were in that class when Scott Melore, pottery prodigy, did a glazing experiment gone wrong. Only I'm staring at the window now, and there's no hint it ever happened.

When Nina vanished before, it was so surreal. . . . I didn't give much thought to *where* she might have gone until I saw her at the diner. Then I figured the disappearing act was part of a cruel joke.

But what if this strange green light really *does* go somewhere else?

I need to settle this once and for all.

I step all the way in, and I'm immersed in green. Everything is so bright—but it doesn't burn my eyes. In this glow, it's like I can see *more* than is visible in regular light. Not because it's brighter, but it seems to penetrate deeper. Like I can see my arm *and* comprehend what it's made of—and understand the space it takes up.

It feels like I'm breathing electricity.

I glance up to get my bearings, and a wave of panic crashes in. I can't see the pole.

I turn around. All the way, I think, but I'm disoriented. All I see is bright light. My heart feels like it's going to explode. I wonder how sweat will react with electric air. I wonder if I'm in some kind of open-air magnetic field that's cooking my brain. Maybe this is the light people see in near-death experiences. It doesn't really hurt, but they never say it does. I try not to breathe.

I'm okay with death if it means seeing Viv again.

I close my eyes and everything goes dark . . . familiar. Like I'm home in bed, drifting off to sleep. I force myself to inhale, ignoring the tingling deep inside my lungs. I reach out. My hands grasp air, but I suck in another breath and take a step. Then another.

I move randomly from side to side until my fingers brush something like . . . wood. I open my eyes. The splintered, dead wood of the pole is right in front of me. I fling my body at it, *out* of the green light, stumble and catch myself with both arms around the sturdy fixture. It's solid; I'm safe. But it still takes a few minutes before the electricity leaves my skin and I can pry myself away.

The green light is gone and I'm in the dark again, staring at the pole, at the shrine.

Or where it ought to be.

A tattered white ribbon hangs in a knot tied around the middle. There are some torn scraps of paper, a couple dead flower petals

on the sidewalk, and part of a card that says *Forever in our hearts.*
There isn't a single picture. I tear the cheerleading shot out of my
pocket and move clockwise, studying the pole, but there's nothing
else there, no trace of the rest of Viv's memorial.

I look down at the photo in my hand and inhale sharply when
I see Viv's smile. How long has it been since I breathed?

Long enough to take down a shrine?

That's impossible. . . . That's sick.

Even Logan wouldn't do that.

Maybe that green energy evaporated everything.

But why not me?

A breeze comes up, chilling my body and clearing my head.

Nina's words haunt me again. *This looks like home. . . .*

My gut twists. In front of me the school is dark, but familiarly
shaped. I force myself to look at the pole again, at the remnants
of cards and ribbon, then beyond it, at the art-room window—
intact. I swallow hard. My eyes dart around, searching for
something else, something safe and recognizable. The bus shelter
sits dirty and abandoned on the opposite corner. At my feet, the
bushes are still misshapen from the car accident.

I cover my mouth, but I can't close my eyes.

E L E V E N

NINA LIVES ON GENESEE STREET. I REMEMBER THINKING THAT WAS odd because Mike lives on Genesee Street and he didn't seem to know her at the diner. But she's the only other person I *know* who has been through that light, so she's the only one who might be able to tell me why things are wrong... I hope. When I get to Genesee Street, I can't recall her exact address. Twenty-six? Twenty-four? I walk slowly up the black asphalt, pausing at Mike's house, number 17.

It looks exactly the way his house has always looked. I keep going.

I stand in front of number 24 a long time. It resembles all the other houses on the street. Split-level, nondescript, dark. I think about Nina saying she was chased away from her friend's house. I think about Viv's missing shrine.

I trip up the uneven front walk, trying to decide what I'll do if this is the wrong house. Do I run? Try to explain? I have no idea what time it is, either too late or too early. I'm halfway to the door when something catches my eye—a light in a window at number 26. It's turned on downstairs, at the back of the house. I glance at the dark front steps ahead of me, and back to the glowing window next door. At least if I try there first, I won't be dragging anyone out of bed.

I cut across the lawns to the neighboring walkway, all the way to the front door. But when I place my thumb over the doorbell, I second-guess myself. What if this isn't her house and I'm about to harass some random family? What if she *is* here? Will she act like she knows me? Pretend not to? I won't let her get away with that this time.

I'm startled by a loud chime inside the house. I pull my hand away from where I leaned too hard against the doorbell.

Run? Explain?

It's an eternal moment before I hear shuffling inside, and I realize how stupid this is. It must be three, maybe four o'clock in the morning, and I'm ringing a stranger's doorbell. If it were my house, I wouldn't answer, or if I did—

The deadbolt slides inside the door.

I swallow, step back.

The door opens a crack, and someone peers out.

The porch light comes on, and I blink against the glare. The brown eye staring up at me widens. There's a gasp. A handheld video game clatters to the floor.

"Owen, what are you—" a girl's voice says.

The door swings open and Nina stares at me, open-mouthed.

"Cam—"

She's not wearing an apron. She isn't laughing. And she isn't green. Her eyes are like saucers. There's a kid in pajamas holding the door open. He looks about ten and he's white as a sheet. She glances at him like she just realized he's there, and closes the door in my face.

So far this is going better than it did at the diner.

I hear murmuring voices through the wood, and when the door finally opens again, Nina's alone. She turns the porch light off, glances up and down the street, and ushers me through the door. She turns the deadbolt once I'm inside, looks at me like I've got the plague or something, then lunges for the light switch. The dim entryway goes black. She sweeps in front of me, brushing my arm. I jerk away—and feel dumb. She's tugging at these lacy curtains on either side of the door, but the moon is shining through the windows so brightly, I don't know why she bothers.

She stops and stares at me like she's evaluating some problem. I'm shivering, but I don't think it's because of the cold. I can't shake the memory of her at the diner, the pitying look in her eyes. Pity for a stranger.

"Tell me what's going on," I demand.

"What?"

"What *is* that green light thing? What does it do? And what's with pretending you didn't know me at the diner?"

She starts to speak—but I cut her off.

81

"How did you know my name before I ever met you? If you live on Mike's street, why don't you go to our school?" I think about the tattered ribbon on the empty pole. "And what the fuck is with taking down my girlfriend's memorial?"

Nina glances up the stairs to a darkened hallway. She hustles wordlessly out of the room, and I follow her to the source of the only light in the house—the kitchen. She closes the door behind me, and we're in a yellow room. Yellow cabinets, yellow counters . . . even these white-and-yellow plastic chairs that look like they belong in a spaceship conference room. She crosses the room and closes the door to another narrow staircase.

"I don't want my brother to hear you," she snaps. "You've scared him enough."

I notice for the first time that she's fully dressed in jeans and a sweater. Either she's up ridiculously early or she hasn't been to bed tonight.

"What's the matter with him?"

She hesitates. "He's sick. I just got him settled down again when—you showed up." She throws her hands in the air. "Why did you come through?"

I blink. I shouldn't have to justify anything to her, she should be the one explaining things to me.

"Do you even know where you are?" she asks.

"I know I'm at the point I want to hit something. Bad."

"No, please don't." She closes her eyes and rubs her forehead with one hand. "Look, right now, you're in my house—which is not my house where you came from. I don't really understand why, but it's like . . . where you're from and where I'm from are the same. Except different."

A door in the front of the house slams.

Nina's head jerks toward the closed kitchen door.

"Owen?" she calls.

"Just me," a woman's voice answers. "You're up early."

Keys are tossed on a table. I hear shuffling like a jacket or boots being removed. Nina turns a panicked face to me. She grabs my arm and tries to shove me toward the back door. I plant my feet. She pushes harder, but her size is nothing against an ex–football star.

"Get out of here!" she hisses.

"Who is that?"

"Just—get out, get out—please!"

Nina can't get me to the back door fast enough, but when she yanks on the scuffed brass knob, it doesn't budge. Her hand moves automatically to the deadbolt, but there's no key. She fumbles over an empty hook on the wall. I pull on the door a couple times myself, as if the right amount of urgency is the combination for the lock. In the front hall, the woman starts hacking a phlegmy smoker's cough, coming toward the kitchen.

Nina whirls and looks at me like the police are outside and I'm something she stole. Her eyes dart away, around the room, to a different door she'd closed.

"Up the stairs!" she hisses, dragging me over.

"No way—"

"Aunt Car will be asleep in fifteen minutes—just stay in my room until then."

"Then what?"

I'm already on the second step trying to whisper at her, but the woman's voice—Aunt Car's, I presume—forces me past the landing to the second tier of stairs. I scramble up the last couple of steps into the upstairs hall.

"Owen has to be back in school today, I told you—"

"He will be," Nina insists.

A cabinet door slams. The voice sighs heavily.

"Good. I had a long night. Make sure he gets on the bus. I'm going to bed."

"No, wait, I could—make you pancakes!" Nina's voice rises too high.

"Pancakes?"

"I was going to anyway—for Owen."

The faint smell of burning Pop-Tarts makes its way up the stairs.

"I'm all set." Aunt Car's voice is louder, closer, and it sounds like her mouth is full. "That sugar-free stuff is crap."

Nina yells, "Well, have a good sleep—*upstairs!*"

Heavy footsteps climb toward me. I back away from the stairs. There are two doors to my right, both closed. There's an open room across from them, next to a bathroom. The hall disappears around a corner that leads I-don't-know-where. Only one door could be the wrong choice, the aunt's room. I dive for the only one that's open.

It latches behind me with a click.

The footsteps reach the top of the steps, and there's a pause. I hear someone chewing loudly, coming closer to the door.

I hold my breath.

A door opens and closes across the hall. I slump against the wood.

Someone coughs behind me and I spin around.

Owen is sitting on a bedspread decorated with footballs and yard lines. He's got the video game in his hands again, but he's lost interest in it. He's staring at me like I'm some kind of freak.

"Sorry . . . wrong room," I whisper. I reach for the door, but hesitate. There's no way Nina's aunt's asleep yet, and I'm not sure what will happen if I get caught. I glance back to the kid, who still looks completely spooked. "Uh, mind if I hang here for a sec?"

His mouth opens a little, but he shakes his head. His hair is darker than his sister's, but they have the exact same brown eyes and freckled nose.

"Thanks."

I rub my knee and look around. This is just awkward. There's an old TV at the foot of the bed and posters from various pro teams on the walls, though they seem weighted toward the Cowboys. A few Pee Wee trophies dot the bookshelf. I used to have a bunch just like them.

"Guess you like football," I mutter.

Something lights up in the kid's flat eyes.

"I've been working on my deep pass," he says with some hesitation. "Throwing from the hips, like you said."

Like I said?

"Yep, that's . . . what you're supposed to do," I say, glancing away from him.

If he doesn't close his mouth and blink pretty soon, I'm out of here. I don't care who sees me.

"So . . . did it hurt?" he asks.

I tear my eyes from his posters. No one has ever asked me that except Viv. My mind flashes school colors, red and white, then blue and orange—*it's wide open, my feet are flying*—*then impact*. I rub the scar above my knee.

"Yeah. It hurt."

The door bursts open, hitting me in the shoulder blade.

"Ow!"

"Shhhh!" Nina hisses. "What are you doing in here? I said *wait in my room*."

I hold my palms face up. "I didn't—"

"You okay, O?" Nina interrupts, turning to her brother, concerned. "Sorry about this, give me fifteen minutes . . . best pancakes you ever had. You okay?"

"I'm fine." His face reddens. "Leave me alone."

"Fifteen minutes," she promises, pushing me back toward the door.

He ignores her and looks at me. "Cam?"

"Yeah . . . ?"

"It doesn't hurt anymore?"

Nina drags me out of the room before I can answer. She clicks the door gently shut behind us and leads me to one of the closed doors across the hall.

She's holding my hand. I pull out of her grasp as she turns the knob. She looks back in surprise for a second, but then raises one finger to her lips and points to the next room. A low, rumbling snore rises and falls through the walls. I follow her into a bare white room.

The bed is neatly made, covered in a plain white bedspread. There's a worn dresser by the closet, a small desk with nothing on it but a couple of pens in a mug. A red beanbag chair sits in the corner under a window next to a precisely arranged bookshelf. There are no clothes on the floor. Not even a pair of shoes. I'm afraid to touch anything.

Viv's room was always messy like mine—well, maybe not quite as bad as it is now. Her one chair was always heaped with clothes she designated "not clean *or* dirty." She tacked photographs and magazine ads all over the walls, interspersed with quotes and phrases she picked up in books, movies, or other people's conversations.

Nina's walls are blank, perfectly white, like a cell. Her bedroom feels more like a guest room, like no one really lives here. There are marks on her mirror as if she used to have pictures taped to it. On one shelf there's a small photograph in a frame that looks like one of those red British phone booths. The picture is of a man and woman with a baby and a little girl. She has copper hair and a great big smile just like Nina did at the diner.

"How come your little brother acts like he knows me?" I ask.

"What?" She looks out the window, away from me.

"How come Owen acts like he knows me—and you act like you know me—except you didn't last night at the restaurant?"

She doesn't say anything, just keeps staring out the window.

"Look, I'm not even mad anymore," I lie. "I just want to know why."

Nina finally turns around and there are tears in her eyes.

"You're my . . . best friend."

This I'm unprepared for. I hesitate, unsure of what to say—I'd never even met this girl before last week. She wipes her face and her expression goes blank again, emotionless, like she's regaining some kind of militant self-control. She takes a deep breath.

"Look, you went through the green light, right?"

"I was in it," I say. "What *is* it, anyway—"

"Did anyone see you?"

"What does it matter?"

"It matters, Cam—did anyone see you?"

"Who cares?"

She makes this noise, and at first I think she's laughing, but she brushes her hair away from her face and I notice her hand is trembling. Her eyes are so serious, I wish I could look away.

"*This* Fayetteville already has a Cam," she says.

I let that sink in, and my skin seems to tingle all over again.

"So you can't—just, it would be bad—if someone saw you." Her whisper sinks so low, I have to read the last part off her lips.

I remember her in my kitchen, going on hysterically about her house not being hers. Then I think about the boarded-up art-room window at the school. The one I saw tonight that looked like it had never even been damaged. I wait for her to blink or twitch or *something*. She finally blinks.

"*This* Fayetteville?" I echo.

She slips past me to her bedside table and starts digging through the drawer. My gaze wanders out the window for reassurance, to the houses on Genesee Street. They look just like they should, like they always have. How could it be different? She pulls something out and slides the drawer closed.

"This was just last summer, out at the lake." She hands me a photograph.

My stomach drops.

It's us. Me and Nina, laughing, holding a fish at least three feet long. She's got one end of it and I have the other; our free arms are around each other. I pull the image closer to my face, looking for signs it's been Photoshopped, but if it has, I can't tell. I recognize the shoreline in the background. I could draw the pine trees along that ridge with my eyes closed. We have a boat out there—*had*, before Dad left—I spot the blue-and-white bow over Nina's shoulder in the picture. The dock stretches out behind us. I can almost hear the sound of water lapping under the planks.

"That's not possible," I say, forgetting to whisper. "I haven't been to the lake in two years. Dad sold that boat when he and my mom divorced."

"He canceled the sale . . . when you called him," she says.

I shake my head. "No way, and besides, I only went there with my—"

"Viv was still your girlfriend," she says softly. I stare at her wordlessly. Her face flushes. "I told you . . . you're my best friend."

Nina's got that awkward look everyone gets now when they slip up and say Viv's name in front of me.

I breathe deeply and look down at the photograph, at myself... can I call him me? His hair is shorter, the way I used to cut it so my football helmet fit. He's grinning like an idiot. Nina's smile is wide too.

I blink. "How?"

"I don't understand it either, but Cam—"

"There are *not* two of me!"

She grits her teeth. "No, there aren't. You're *you* . . . in your own world."

My own world? My world . . . all I can think is I want to go home—where Viv's shrine is still up and my dad no longer owns a boat. I reach for the doorknob.

Nina flies between me and the door. "What I'm trying to say is—you *can't* go out there right now. You saw me last night, right? Only it wasn't me?"

I envision her wearing that green diner apron, scrunching up her freckles when she smiled. My skin feels clammy.

"I think so . . ."

Her voice is shaking now. "What was she like?"

"She looked just like you."

She gives a hard smile and steps closer. I can see the same sprinkle of freckles on her nose, but they don't move. "And she acted just like me too?"

I shake my head. "No."

"How was she different?"

I think for a moment. "She seemed more . . . cheerful. Or something."

Her face darkens. "See? You could tell it wasn't me. Just like everyone here will know you're not our Cam."

I think about seeing Nina for the first time, and wonder how I might've reacted to a transparent green version of myself instead. I shove my hand in my pocket and touch Viv's picture.

"Then I should get back," I say.

"Look, you do have to go back. But if you leave right now, someone might see you go through."

I glance out the window, catching the beginning of a light pink sunrise. By the time I get back to the school, it'll be full daylight.

"If I hurry—"

"It's too late."

She crosses her arms in front of her, and it's so stupid because I could easily push by, whether I'm in shape or not. But she has a point about not being seen. I'm not super anxious to run into anyone who might think I'm *him* right now. I look down at the picture of us—them—and rub my jaw, unsure my face is even capable of that expression. All I'm sure of is that I need a shave. I look up at Nina's solemn face. It strikes me again how opposite she is, both of us are, from our other . . . versions. What gives her a job and him a boat neither of us has? Why doesn't she scrunch her freckles when she smiles? What makes him look so damn happy in this picture?

TWELVE

NINA CLOSES THE DOOR AND I LISTEN TO HER PAD DOWNSTAIRS TO get breakfast for her brother. With no one to talk to, my ears tune in to the noise coming through the wall. Aunt Car sounds like a muffled freight train, but as long as she's chugging, no one gets in trouble. I wander to the window. Mike's rust-red Toyota is parked in front of his house down the street—nothing out of the ordinary there. I wander back. I pick a pencil out of the mug and set it sideways on the empty desk. I don't know how Nina stands it in here.

The picture sits facedown on the dresser. I think about telling Dr. Summers the good news: I'm perfectly sane—the *world* has gone crazy. Worlds? I wish I'd taken physics or paid more attention in math or something. I lift the edge of the photo and peer at the other me. Trying to wrap my brain around this is giving me a headache.

I wander around the room, but the crazy tidiness makes it difficult to be nosy. A beat-up rag doll sits on the bed, but even its arms are neatly folded in its lap. The closet door is ajar, so I peek in. It smells like cedar. Nina's clothes hang arranged by length in a scheme of mostly boring dark colors. I notice a stack of framed posters facing the wall just inside the door, and this piques my interest. I pull the first one back to have a look. It's a movie poster from the original *Night of the Living Dead*. I thumb through the other frames and find a ton of classics. *The Pit and the Pendulum*, *Suspiria*, *The Exorcist*, even *Carrie*. I've seen all of these, and loved them—despite Viv hating horror movies. I glance out at the sterile walls of Nina's room and back at the brightly colored movie prints. Weird.

I close the closet door and study the bookshelf's insanely straight rows, which I notice are even alphabetized by author. It's mostly fiction—some contemporary, some classics I recognize from school. I spot a well-used copy of *Ethan Frome*, among others. Maybe Nina can help me study. On the bottom row, a red hardbound volume sticks out past the shelf. I am instantly curious. It's the only book that doesn't conform to the obsessive-compulsive pattern. It's too tall and too wide.

I bend to pull it free, pausing to listen for Nina's returning footsteps. All I hear is snores rising and falling through the drywall. I grasp the spine of the book and slip it off the shelf.

I have to admit I'm interested. Is there another Logan West in this place? I grimace. Maybe he looks like the douche he truly is in all his pictures . . . maybe I'll discover more about my BFF Nina—maybe I'll see Viv. My heart picks up until I recall the tattered shrine and mangled bushes by the utility pole in *this* world. I have to close my eyes until they stop stinging. Things here are more worthlessly the same than they are different. I slide my hand to my pocket, where her yearbook cheerleading picture is, but that was taken when we were freshmen. This is last year's book, junior year. Neither one of us is going to be in it anyway.

I flip pages randomly. Some are black-and-white, some in color. Rows and rows of faces alternate with magazine-like spreads about LIFE AT FOWLER HIGH.

I stop flipping.

There's Viv. In full color.

Her smile is so wide it seems to cut across the page. She stands in a silky red gown that rides her body as if she was sewn into it. People lean in close to her on either side. Paper hearts dot the air. There's a tiara in her piled-up black hair. She stands under a banner that reads VALENTINE'S DAY DANCE, RED KING AND QUEEN, holding the arm of a stiff-looking guy in a tux.

I blink.

It's me.

I sink into the beanbag chair and try to make out the other faces—Tash Clemons in pink, Nikita Roberts in white. They stand close to Viv, like her attendants or something. Mike lurks in a shadow to my right; a bunch of people crowd together below the stage. Everyone's grinning just as big as Viv. The headache I've been harboring breaks loose inside my skull. My vision blurs.

But we don't go to dances . . .

I slam the book closed.

I grip the hardbound edges of the yearbook, as if the pressure might change what I saw inside—Viv and me at a dance we never attended, crowned the Red Queen and King by everyone we hate? I tear it open again and slash through the pages, searching for *something* familiar—something true. Logan's overdimpled grin sails by and I thumb back to that photo more carefully. It's on a two-page spread devoted to Rams football.

The caption under the pic reads: *Varsity Captains.* On the field in full pads and uniforms are Logan West and Rashad Davis, last year's senior star running back. They're on the field, helmets in hand, kneeling on either side . . . of *me.*

All I can do is stare.

I'm in our red-and-white uniform holding a ball, smiling like a moron. Someone must have posed the shot, because not only is Logan kneeling at my feet, but I look like I own the field. My stomach twists—but I remember to breathe—until a headline at the top of the page catches my eye:

FOWLER QUARTERBACK OVERCOMES DEVASTATING
INJURY FOR RECORD JUNIOR YEAR

I try to swallow, but my mouth is bone dry. I skim the article, eyes darting over the other pictures. *Camden Pike . . . right leg shattered . . . last year's Homecoming game . . .* There's a shot of me running, looking over my shoulder, not seeing the linebacker headed my way at full speed. I recognize the last moment of my last game, and cover my eyes.

I pull my aching knee to my chest.

One moment, that's all it took. My life stopped rotating around schedules and practices and became a haze of pain between doses of morphine. They said I'd walk again, but the season went on without me. Sometimes the team even won with Logan. I didn't matter. Nothing mattered anymore.

I run a shaky hand around the captain photo—I'm afraid to touch it.

Between my fingers I catch a glimpse of Viv on the sideline, all pom-poms and ponytail, filling out her uniform in ways I'm *too* familiar with. The dull ache moves from my leg into my groin.

"Hey, I thought I'd see if you were hungry—"

Nina stops short when she sees the book in my lap. She closes the door.

"That's my yearbook," she says.

"It's definitely not mine."

She leans against the door awkwardly.

"It's funny . . ." I get up and hold the picture in front of her face.

"*Your* best friend is the team captain, he's the freaking Red King, and his cheerleader girlfriend was the envy of the school—"

"Keep your voice down," Nina hisses.

"Is this why you didn't want me roaming the streets?" I ask. "Afraid I might run into someone when I'm *so* not him?"

My knee throbs. I stare at her hard, but she won't look at me, won't speak. I push past her for the door.

"You can't leave—"

"Fuck it."

"No, my aunt!"

I'm out of her bedroom and halfway down the hall when I hear a door open behind me and a sleepy voice call, "Nina, what are you— But that looked like—"

I'm down the stairs and outside before I can hear her reply.

The chill is still in the outdoor air, but it looks like the sun might make its way out of the clouds. I spit on the front walk on my way out. At the corner of Genesee Street I realize I'm still holding Nina's yearbook. I consider chucking it into someone's yard, but I turn it over, study the red leather cover, and tuck it under my arm instead. I'm not ready to let go of anything that holds a picture that beautiful of Viv, no matter how fucked up it was to see. She looked happier than I've ever seen her—on the arm of her star quarterback. My stomach sinks at that thought and I bite my lip hard to remember to breathe. I scan the street, but don't see anyone coming, which is too bad because I'm telling whoever I run into to fuck the hell off. The other me can deal with it. His life is charmed enough.

THIRTEEN

THERE'S A SMUDGE ON MY BEDROOM CEILING THAT LOOKS A LITTLE like Jupiter, complete with a large red spot. I've been staring at it all day, since I forced myself back through the creepy green light and made it home. I'm pretty sure if I keep watching, it'll start orbiting my room.

Today, that wouldn't seem so weird.

My phone rings, directly in my ear. I fumble under the pillow, paw through the unmade sheets next to my head.

"Hello?"

"Camden? Where are you? Your shift started twenty minutes ago."

I glance out the window. It's almost dusk.

"Shit."

"Excuse me?"

"Sorry, sir, I . . ."

I peer across the room at my closet and try to think of an excuse. A few shirts are hanging, but most of my clothes spill out onto the floor, avalanche-style. A white sleeve sticks up like a flag of surrender toward the back. A white jersey with a red number five emblazoned on it. My grip tightens on the phone. The *other* me somehow wore that number again.

"I quit."

I hang up. Turn the phone off. It's much easier to blow people off when you don't have to hear their nagging voices.

I shove the pile of clothes inside the closet and lean against the door so I don't have to see that red-and-white jersey, or think about him. How could I—*he*—be playing football? We couldn't have had the same injury; maybe that's the difference. The pain was . . . I was so doped, I can't remember the pain. But the first day they made me try physical therapy, just trying to *walk* was harder than any practice Coach Reed ever dealt.

The doctors said it was unlikely I could play again. *Unlikely*—don't bother, kid, your career is over. Viv was there. She held my hand when they said it. I made it till everyone left before I finally broke down, and she climbed carefully into the bed with me. She brushed back my hair, shaggier than it had been in a while, and told me she liked it better long. Then she put her cheek against mine and reassured me, *Who needs football as long as we have each other?*

She stayed there by my side, every day and night, while everything around us went to total shit. Dad left that month. Mom

99

turned into a bigger workaholic zombie. The team lost the season without me.

But I still had Viv.

Nina's yearbook lies at the foot of the bed. I open it to the picture of the Red King and Queen, and trace my fingertip over Viv's beauty-queen smile. She only gave up cheering when I left football. I don't think she realized choosing me over them would cost her her friends. But . . . this . . . it's like the picture restores her rightful place in the universe.

I wonder if she was happier this way.

Sometime around ten my stomach wakes me up. I crank my iPod and try to ignore the unhappy growls, but after a while it feels like it's starting to gnaw on itself, so I stumble out to the kitchen. The whole house is dark. No car in the driveway. Mom either passed out at the office, or she's working late. There's no note in the fruit bowl.

I get out the Toasty O's box, but there are only a couple of stale O's at the bottom. I dig around in the pantry and fridge until I find some frostbitten waffles at the back of the freezer behind some trout in a Ziploc bag from the last time Dad and I went to the lake. Definitely expired. I toast the yellow discs until they're chewy, slather them with peanut butter, which never seems to go bad, and head back to my bed.

Halfway across the living room, I notice the message light blinking on the cordless phone. I suck peanut butter off my fingers and listen to a voice message from the secretary at school complaining about my absence, one from my newly *ex*-boss, and two from Dad that I delete without listening. I clear the call log and go back to the fruit bowl.

Mom—
Stayed home sick. Feeling better.
Might need a note tomorrow.
Cam

I toss the yearbook under the bed and flop down. My sheets smell kind of ripe. I fell asleep in my jeans before, and now they're digging into my crotch. I strip to my boxers, flip my pillow over, and try not to think. Not about green lights, or Nina, football, Viv—or anything else that might have been. I cue my iPod to something with lots of bass and no words.

I'm almost asleep when the drums start thumping too hard, out of sync with the beat. It's annoying because I like this song, but just as quickly as it started, it stops. I roll against the wall, but it starts up again, thumping in my ears . . . and straight through my shoulder. I hit pause. The beat repeats, rapping on the window above my head in an urgent pattern: 4-2-3. My blood chills.

It's how Viv and I always used to announce our visits.

I throw the curtain aside—and see Nina's face through the glass. My lungs release; air flows in and out of my chest again.

Always Nina, never Viv.

I let go of the sheet I've balled up in my fist, growing steadily more annoyed than freaked out. I open the window.

"What do you want?"

"We need to talk. Let me in."

"Why bother with me? Why don't you go talk to *him*?"

She closes her eyes. "Just let me in."

"Nobody gets through this window without at least two cigarettes," I say. A memory of Viv pulling the curtain back with two between her lips makes me wish I'd never said anything.

Nina ignores me and climbs over the sill onto my bed as if she's done this a few times. She's got on tall brown boots and warm-looking tights, which I can't help noticing when her legs are dangling over my head.

"You don't smoke," she says, standing straight and fixing her skirt.

"Really." I cross my arms. "What else don't *I* do?"

Her face reddens.

I bore my eyes into her the way I used to stare at Viv when I was trying to win a fight. She doesn't last long—she's no Viv.

"God—" she stops. "You're different . . . but you're just like him sometimes."

"The guy's got my face, but that's all," I mutter.

I wait for her to sit down to talk, but she just stands there. Her back is straight, like she's preparing to give a speech. My eyes follow hers to the overturned desk chair, defunct stereo, and pile of crap burying the laptop on my desk. She stands on the one empty spot of green carpet on the floor, although on closer inspection, I realize it's littered with crumbs. Her eyes drift to me, then back to the floor. I wish I had a shirt on. And that I'd changed the sheets.

"Look," she says. "I only came here to tell you not to go through—that thing again. It's not safe." She rubs her hands like she's trying to brush off an unpleasant sensation.

"The green-light thing?" I ask. "I wasn't planning on it. . . ."

"Good," she says stiffly. "I don't know what it is or how it got there, but it just seems like something we shouldn't mess with . . . more."

I narrow my eyes. "You came through it just to tell me that?"

"Yeah. . . ." She hesitates, then moves abruptly for the window. "Okay, good-bye."

"Wait—" I grab her arm, and both of us stare at my hand in surprise. I let go fast. "There's something I need to know."

"The less you know, the better," she says through her teeth.

"You haven't even let me ask yet—"

"Trust me, you don't need to."

Frigid air pours through the open window, giving me goosebumps, but it's probably the only thing going for the state of my room. I spot my black hoodie wedged between the wall and the bed, pull it free, and yank it over my head. Nina's watching when I look up. Her cheeks turn pink as I work it down over my chest. I glance away, gesturing for her to sit in the overturned desk chair. She doesn't move. Her eyes are flat. I hate that I can't tell what she's thinking the way I always could with Viv.

I slide out of bed, shake the chair free of an old pair of jeans, and set it right again.

"Please?" I say.

She sighs. "What do you want to know?"

I drop back on the bed, grateful my boxers are clean at least.

"I haven't been able to play football since—my injury." Saying it out loud makes my throat sting. "So . . . how did *he*?"

She rubs the side of her head, considering.

"He wasn't going to," she says slowly. "After he met with the doctors about it, he gave up."

I lean forward. That sounds about right. . . .

"But then what? What happened?"

"I don't know." She shrugs. "He changed his mind."

"Something had to be different—he wasn't hurt badly?"

She shakes her head, paces a couple steps, and sinks into the desk chair. Her face remains blank, except she keeps pursing her mouth like she's weighing what she should or shouldn't say.

"No, it was bad. He and Owen shared a room at the hospital— I was there," she says, looking me in the eye. "It was just . . . one day he'd given up, and the next . . . I came in to see Owen, and both of you—*them*—were sitting up in bed, talking pigskin."

"Owen? In the hospital?"

"He's diabetic," Nina mumbles. "He was really sick."

Something's still not adding up. I study her, looking for some kind of clue. She twists the edge of her skirt, but her eyes are still trained on mine.

"Hmm. So you're my best friend and you have no idea how I went back to football?"

"No . . . I didn't know you as well then." Her cheeks go pink again. "But I do know that when you make up your mind to do something—" She pauses. "I've never seen anything like it."

I stare at my open palms. My dad used to say something like that about me. But this guy, this *me*, still goes to the lake with Dad. He's the captain of the team. I try to envision the Red King in that hospital room . . . but all I see is me. There was an empty bed behind a curtain. . . . Mom slept there a few nights before going back to work. Dad sat on it awkwardly and offered me Jell-O. Viv always climbed into my bed. No one else ever came in, especially not Nina's brother.

"He's really into football—Owen?"

"When he gets to high school, he wants to be just like—" She stops.

We both look away. If there's one thing I'm sure of, that kid will never want to be me.

She rises and goes to the window again. "I have to get back to him . . . good-bye, Cam."

"But wait, aren't you dying to find out all about the other *you*?"

She turns. "Not really."

I stare at her, but I still can't read her. This has to be an act. Who wouldn't want to know how their life could be different?

"Well, I'm going to guess you don't work at a diner . . . but that's where I saw you. Running around, filling orders—service with a great big smile."

I wait for her to react, maybe laugh at how different she sounds, but she just stands in the freezing cold by the window and doesn't move.

"She's not me."

"You don't go to my school, if you're wondering—"

"I don't want to know."

"You're not even a little curious?"

As soon as I say it, I realize . . . *I'm* curious. What makes the Nina in front of me so somber when the girl I saw at the diner was all smiles and so eager to please? What's different? If Camden Pike has everything in her world, shouldn't she?

"Look, I have to get back. Owen's waiting for me," she says. "You really won't go through the light again . . . ?"

I don't speak, just shake my head.

"Okay," she says. "I just wanted . . . to say good-bye."

She comes toward me, hesitates, then puts her boot on the bed and climbs over me, her long hair swishing over my arm. She swings her legs out the window and her feet crunch dry leaves when she hops to the ground. I sit up, wanting to say something else. Maybe ask where her parents are, or why she keeps horror movie posters stashed in her closet. But when I look out the window, she's disappeared into the night.

FOURTEEN

DR. SUMMERS WENT ON AND ON ABOUT DEEP BREATHING TODAY, and it was all I could do to keep my butt on her couch and stare at the carpet. When I get home, there's the pizza note in the kitchen again. I shove the money in my pocket and don't bother to write back. I turn on the TV and flip through the guide until I find something about dirt bikes. Nothing like a Friday night alone watching people shred through mud on two wheels.

Except that's not at all what it is. There's this guy hopping around on the rear wheel of his motorcycle, but he's in a city, jumping it onto loading docks and riding over a parked car. He does these insane maneuvers where he propels the whole bike off a ledge, rotates in the air, and manages to land perfectly on the trash-littered pavement. Finally, they show him loading the bike into a service elevator and accelerating out onto the roof of an old brick building. He hops onto the lip of the roof and proceeds to ride all the way around the edge. The camera zooms to the filthy pavement eight stories below, and when it pans back up, the crew has removed the front wheel of his bike. My stomach drops. One wrong move to the left and the guy tumbles to his death on an expensive hunk of metal. But he completes the circuit doing a wheelie, wavering only slightly at the corners, and hops down to huge applause. My palms are covered in sweat.

I guess I'm supposed to be amazed at what the stupid guy accomplished, but all I can think about is what might have happened. What if he got his pants caught and fell off his bike? What if the wind had been different, or he'd made a wrong move? What if *I* had made different choices? If I'd never dropped the lighter—never *took up* smoking in the first place? Would things have changed if I'd met Nina and her brother? Or if Viv had stayed with Logan? What if I'd never quit football and she'd stayed a cheerleader? What would have happened if we'd never even met? Would she still be here, happy and alive?

I wish I'd never opened Nina's stupid yearbook.

I click the TV off and go to my room.

Maybe the Other Cam's life isn't as great as it looked. . . . Surely the guy had some kind of flaw. Perfect life, perfect team, perfect girlfriend—my breath cuts off, my eyes burning as I remember the tattered remnants of memorial on his side.

He *did* do things differently, and he lost her anyway.

But he couldn't have appreciated her. Not the way I did.

I turn my light on and kneel to scan the random items that have collected like driftwood under my bed. I spot my old earbuds wrapped around a foul-looking sock, and tug the whole mess gently out by the cord. Along with my school ID from freshman year, a chopstick, a blank CD, and lots of dust, comes the red leather yearbook. I drop onto the bed and open the cover.

There's a picture of Fowler High, in all its 1960s architectural splendor. The address is below that, but the rest of the paper is blank. I go to turn the page when something catches my eye. On the inside flap, crammed down in the corner, is something handwritten.

I peer at it more closely . . . and recognize my own writing.

So the guy's got my face *and* my handwriting. Great.

N—
You saved my life.
—C

I read the note again. Nina saved me? From what? I read the words a third time, but they still don't make sense. I shattered my leg in the Homecoming game, but there was no chance I was going to die. The only time I came close—

I swallow hard and flip through the pages in the rest of the yearbook, but I don't find any other writing. I skip past the Valentine's Day Dance spread because I can't bear to see Viv in that dress again. There's an index of names in the back, with a page number for every time someone appears in a photo. I skip past

Pike and Hayward, each followed by a string of numbers, until I find LARSON, NINA—PAGE 32.

The pages stick together as I thumb back to the rows of juniors . . . but I find her, second row down, looking into the camera like the photographer told her to *Smile!* and she just can't summon the effort. At least one thing in this book is familiar. Despite her expression, it's actually a nice picture. Her hair looks different in black-and-white—it's lighter. Her mouth is serious, but not somber. I find myself wishing I knew her better, or even understood how we became friends.

I close the book and sit with my palms pressed to my eyes until a swirl of color rises up behind my lids.

I get dressed.

I never actually said I wouldn't go through the green glow again. I'm concealed behind the shrine, working up the nerve to stick my hand into the night air. I glance at the boarded-up art-room window—the one that most definitely hasn't been replaced yet—and bite my lip. Nina's right, it probably isn't something we should mess with . . . but I need to know what the note means. I would never have written it, so why would he? What happened?

Passing through strange, otherworldly light is a hell of a lot easier when you know what's waiting on the other side. The electricity buzzing through my skin only makes me slightly nauseous this time, though I have to duck a little to fit through the space, and I don't remember having to do that before.

I crouch by the bushes and let my stomach settle. Nina's

yearbook is tucked under my left arm. I turn, trying to get oriented to my surroundings . . . make sure I am where I think I am. But the art-room window is now miraculously intact again, and there's no more than a trace of Viv's shrine. I touch the dirty white ribbon tied around the pole, and it falls to the ground in a limp ring. There's part of a candle stub left on the pavement, some scraps of paper stapled to the wood. You can tell there was a memorial here, but you'd never know who it was for.

If *he* showed up right now, I'd beat the shit out of him. Viv died on this spot, and he can't even honor her memory by maintaining her shrine? I'm disgusted with myself for wanting what he had. Overcoming a debilitating injury, salvaging his reputation, his career—what's any of it worth if he took the most important thing he had for granted?

Blood roars in my ears and I'm consumed by this need to hold Viv against me, so she can feel the constant ache that courses through my body, that hasn't left since I saw all that blood and shattered glass. *I* want her back. *I* live with the emptiness of her absence. *He* doesn't even miss her!

I grip the yearbook tightly and start walking toward Nina's house as fast as I can. If he's her best friend, I want to know why. I want to know why she bothered saving the asshole's life.

I'm halfway up Euclid when I stop at the corner of Belleview. Viv's street. I can picture her house, long and white, second from the last. There were juniper bushes outside her window. My feet turn and I'm walking. I could get there with my eyes closed. I just want to see it, be near something that proves she was here.

I have no idea what time it is, but the street is mostly dark. There's a TV on here, a porch light there, but I don't hear any cars, or even dogs barking. I don't have to look up to know when I'm in front of Viv's house. Freshman year, the city poured a new sidewalk and we snuck out in the middle of the night to draw our initials in the cement: V.H. + C.P. The letters are under my feet. From this spot I can see Viv's window, but not the front door, behind a large willow tree. If she gave me the all-clear, I used to climb in or help her out without either of us being seen. I think her parents liked me fine, but it was faster this way. No small talk or reminders of curfew, just the two of us, alone.

I lift my head.

There's a light in her window.

For a second, my heart stops.

My chest hurts thinking of someone poking around in her room. Are they cleaning it out? Converting it into an office? A guest bedroom? I imagine Viv's room being dismantled—her favorite quotes and pictures peeled off the walls. I feel sick. I wonder if her scent still lingers on her clothes. I'm halfway across the lawn before I can think.

I creep carefully into the juniper so no one will see me from inside. I haven't seen Mr. and Mrs. Hayward since the funeral. . . . I was hoping we'd never have to see each other again.

Someone is in there, on her bed.

I move to the corner of the window and peer in.

My breath catches in my throat. There's a girl sitting with her back to me on Viv's bed. She's thin, and her black hair is held back with a red ribbon. She's hunched over on the phone, tracing circles with her finger on the quilt. Every now and then she nods, but if she's speaking, it's too low to hear through the glass. She's wearing red and white, her long legs tucked beneath a short pleated skirt.

She nods quickly a few more times, then drops the phone to her side and flips it closed. She wipes her face. After a moment, she swings her legs over the side of the bed and starts to undress. The outfit is a Red Rams cheerleading getup. She strips it off, adding the top and skirt to a pile on the one chair in the room, exchanging them for a rumpled pair of pink pajamas. There's a small brown birthmark on one side of her lower back. It looks like a little diamond—I know without having to get a closer look because I used to lay kisses on that spot like it was the most sacred place on earth. I feel like the world falls away when she turns. The thick black curls that used to tumble down her back swing short at her chin, held back with a red ribbon. Her face is thinner and blotchy, her dark eyes rimmed in red. But the arching eyebrows I used to trace with my thumb are unchanged.

I can't breathe. I watch in a daze as she slips into the pajamas, and there is no doubt left in my mind. I spent three years memorizing every inch of this body, this face, and the last two months aching for one glimpse of her again.

I bang on the glass and scream her name.

"VIV!"

FIFTEEN

I THROW MYSELF AT THE WINDOW, BANGING AND HOLLERING. I DON'T
even know what I'm saying. I can't believe my eyes—I need to get
to her, touch her, *hold* her.

She jumps back from the bed, gripping a blanket in her hands.
Her eyes dart around the room, but when they settle on the shaking window pane, I grin.

"VIV! Viv, it's me! It's ME!" I'm pushing at the window, but
it's latched, so I just hop up and down like a moron.

Her dark eyes meet mine. Her face goes bedsheet white.

She pulls the blanket to her chest, backing into the wall. Her
lips barely move, and I think I make out my name, but I can't
really tell what she's saying until her mouth stops forming words
and opens in a scream.

The sound pierces through the glass, through my chest, and

it's like I'm knocked into the shadows. Her father forces through the door seconds later, looking just as panicked as Viv, who has crumpled in a heap on the floor, trembling. Mrs. Hayward comes in seconds after her husband, and kneels by Viv, who's holding her knees, shaking her head and crying.

My brain feels thick; my limbs heavy. I stare at Viv's inky curls while her mom rubs her back. She lifts her head and peers tentatively over her knees out the window. I know she can't see me now where I stand, but disappointment wars with relief in her eyes. Mr. Hayward's voice booms and he strides purposefully out of the room. The outdoor lights come on, illuminating the lawn, and adrenaline surges through my veins. All I want to do is rush inside, pull Viv into my arms, and tell her she's safe now; we'll never be parted again. But something in her haunted face glues me to the shadows. The front door slams and every instinct I have shrieks for me to leave.

Didn't she see it's *me*? Why would she scream?

"Who's out there?" Mr. Hayward shouts in my direction.

My feet override my head and I escape through the neighbor's yard. I gasp for air, eyes burning as I run, but though my heart pounds, I'm numb in my chest.

By the time I get to Nina's house, my eyes are swollen and I can't breathe through my nose. I collapse on her front porch and slump over, resting my head on the floorboards. I'm vaguely aware of a zombielike sound emanating from my mouth.

Viv's *alive.*

I've dreamed of it a hundred thousand times. But never like this.

A shaft of light slides toward me. Someone gasps.

"Nina!" Owen calls.

Footsteps rush through the house, slow down, and come to a tentative stop near my head. The door closes, and we're in blackness. I peel my face off the porch and wipe my sleeve under my nose.

"Why—" I choke, and have to start again. "Why didn't you tell me?"

I can barely make her out in the moonlight, my eyes are so bleary. She stands perfectly still, back flat against the door.

"Tell you what?" she asks.

"Viv's *alive*?"

Her face pales. In the silence, my head starts to clear. My heart picks up. She kept this from me and now she isn't going to say anything?

"You saw her memorial—you knew!"

"I didn't—"

"Don't *lie* to me anymore, Nina!"

She looks down at me, huddled on the floor, and I swear she gives me the same pitying look she had at the diner.

"Viv is alive here—" Her voice cracks. "Because *you're* the one who died!"

The street gets so silent we could be the only people around for miles. I focus on breathing, but the air seems too thin. I can't get enough of it. I support myself against the house and close my eyes.

Viv's alive . . . and *I died*?

"How?" I whisper.

She pauses. "Hit-and-run. Two months ago—Sunday the fifth."

"Sunday the fifth," I mumble. "Hit-and-run?"

"At the corner by the school," she says.

I try to envision it—the fall of the Red King—but my mind can only handle one gruesome death in that spot on *that* date. A sick feeling creeps into me, slithering through my gut like . . . guilt? I'd made up my mind to hate the other me an hour ago. But did he deserve *that* more than I did?

"Did—" Nina hesitates. "Did Viv see you tonight?"

I open my eyes. "What?"

"I just need to know—did she see your face?"

I think back to the chaos in Viv's room. She'd seen me, all right . . . but in the moments afterward, when she lifted her head, I'm positive she was hoping to see me again.

"What's it to you if she did?" I ask.

"It's everything, Cam—she thinks you're *dead*!"

"So?" I pull myself unsteadily to my feet. "I thought she was dead too, maybe this is meant to be—"

"*No!*"

We both listen in surprise to her voice echoing off the houses.

"She's not what she seems."

Nina steps forward and reaches to touch me, but I pull away. The yearbook I'd been clutching under my arm falls open on the porch with a thud. I bend to pick it up, but she's already kneeling with it in her hands, staring at the open page. She lingers to touch the handwriting—*You saved my life.*

"Guess he was wrong about that," I say.

She looks up at me in surprise, then back at the words. She covers her mouth. My stomach sinks at the look on her face—some unnatural mixture of horror and grief. A feeling I'm too well acquainted with. I wish I could take it back. She slams the book shut and rises to her full petite height.

"Why did you come back?" she demands.

I open my mouth. I used to have an answer for that, but all I can think anymore is *Viv.*

If Viv is alive in this place, that must be why I'm here.

"If you want what's best, for you *and* for her this time . . ." Nina's lips continue to move, but if she's still speaking, I can't make out the words. She shakes her head and raises her voice. "Please, Cam, *please* just go home."

A tear escapes down her cheek. She walks through the front door and shuts it in my face.

I step off the porch, confused. Why wouldn't she tell me Viv was alive? A light in an upstairs window goes out. I kick the grass and start down the path to get away, when the door opens behind me.

I turn around. "You know, just because you want—"

Owen stands alone on the porch in blue pajamas with football helmets all over them.

I wait for him to speak.

He gives a furtive glance over his shoulder and closes the door carefully. I wipe my hand over my face, exhausted, and walk back to the porch. At this point I just want out of here, but I don't think I should leave the kid standing there by himself.

"Shouldn't you be in bed?" I ask.

"Nina really missed you," he says with a tentative smile. "I'm glad you're back."

I hesitate, unsure if he still thinks I'm a ghost or a hero—or if he's figured out I'm neither.

"Look, Owen . . ."

"I wish Mom and Dad would come back too." He stares at the ground.

I swallow hard. "What . . . happened to them?" He looks at me funny. Am I supposed to know about this? "Sometimes it's hard to remember things." I hesitate. "After you come back."

He nods like this makes perfect sense. "They went on vacation and didn't wake up. The police said there was a leak."

It must have been carbon monoxide.

My mom had a case once where a whole family died of carbon-monoxide poisoning because of some pipe in their basement. They all just went to bed one night and never woke up. The mom, dad, and two kids, even their dog died. I can't imagine losing either of my parents. I'm surprised by the thought, but I know it's true at the same time.

I lower myself to my knees in front of him, and squeeze his shoulder. "I'm sorry, O."

He shrugs. "I was a little kid then."

I glance back up to the darkened window above us, and Owen follows my gaze.

He tilts his head. "When I was really little, Nina used to be a lot more fun. She got nice again after we met you." His smile returns. "That's why I'm glad you're back."

"Yeah . . ." I rise to my feet, uncomfortable. "Me too."

He tiptoes back to the door, but turns.

"Will you stay around, Cam?"

I hesitate, thinking of Nina's bizarre warning, but picturing Viv alive and healthy, alone in her room a few blocks away.

"I might hang out a bit," I say.

I walk down Genesee Street, trying to sort through the jumble of facts in my brain. Nina's parents are dead here, but since she doesn't go to my school and seems so much happier back home, it's a safe guess they're probably alive there. . . . I hurt my leg in *both* places, but here I still played football. Except now I'm dead here, and Viv's dead there. My head reels. Who—or what—decides what will happen? Wouldn't it have been fairer to at least kill me and Viv in the same place? If I had died in the accident with Viv, and he hadn't, Nina wouldn't have had to lose her best friend . . . she might be happier. The other me would have kept doing everything right, and *his* Viv—

I stop short in the middle of the road.

I'm such an idiot. In my head I see her too-thin frame hunched over on the bed, wiping at her blotchy face. No wonder she screamed when she saw me—Viv thinks *I'm* dead.

A dull ache spreads through my chest like a reopening wound. The thought of her suffering the way I have overwhelms me. I don't care anymore who lived and who died—Viv is alive, but she's in pain—because of me.

I start walking, faster, toward the end of the street. I've been trying to tell myself for months that she would have been okay if I'd died. But the grip of her despair was too familiar. Her hunched, hollow form looked too much like the image I've been glaring at in the mirror for two months. I just need to watch her again, make sure she's okay. I up my pace to a jog before reaching the bottom of the hill. If anyone knows how Viv feels right now, it's me.

I break into a run.

SIXTEEN

VIV'S LIGHT IS STILL ON. I FORCE MYSELF TO WAIT ON THE SIDEWALK by our initials until my leg stops throbbing and I'm sure the coast is clear. The outdoor floodlights are on too, but they cast as many parts of the yard into shadow as they illuminate.

There's movement in the window.

I stay perfectly still.

Viv's slender, short-haired silhouette comes into view. She hugs herself, lingering by the glass, profile sweeping back and forth like she's searching for something in the yard. After several minutes, her arms fall to her sides, and she backs away from view.

This is my chance.

I dash across the yard, pausing under the willow tree. There's a half second between there and the window when I have to cross a beam of floodlight, but I'm counting on no one looking out at that exact moment.

I peer in a corner of the window as I did before, heart in my throat. Viv's pacing the room. She's still wearing her pink pajamas, but she's thrown on a too-big Fowler Rams sweatshirt over them. I used to have one just like it. She stops with her back turned. I can't tell what she's doing, but then she shifts a little and I see she's biting her nails. She always does that when she's upset. I scan the room around her, eerily similar to the room I knew . . . and somehow different. It's not messy enough to qualify as a pigsty, since you can actually see a large part of the floor, but since the desk and dresser are mostly obscured, it's a long way from tidy. She still has all her quotes and pictures on the walls, but they're different. There's more glamour, more *people*—fewer pictures of things and places. Over the bed there's a shot of us from the Valentine's Day Dance.

She turns to pace back this way, and glances at the window.

Our eyes meet.

I see her body stiffen, but this time she swallows and doesn't scream.

I feel like I need to offer some cue—let her know it's just me, it's okay—and then I remember. I knock gently on the glass: 4-2-3.

Her shoulders loosen, just barely, but she stays across the room. I push on the window, and this time it slides up. Her big, beautiful dark eyes get a little bigger, but she still hasn't moved or cried out.

There's a notch in the house foundation that has always been just big enough for my foot. I watch Viv carefully before I slip the tip of my shoe into it, hoisting myself to the window ledge. Her room has a window seat inside, but I don't dare come any farther than the sill in case I need to bolt again.

I sit sideways in the window and stare at her. As hard as I've tried to keep her in my memory these last two months, I've still forgotten how beautiful she is. Even in an old sweatshirt, eyes red, hair a mess—it's all I can do not to tear across the room and fold her into my arms.

Her bottom lip trembles. She hasn't moved, but her eyes are shining. She wraps one arm across her waist, bringing her other shaking hand to her mouth. I realize she's at a disadvantage. I know neither of us is a ghost, or a zombie, or whatever—but she doesn't.

I hold my arms out to her.

"It's me," I whisper. "It's okay."

She draws in a sharp breath, but it's like some threshold is broken. She crosses the room, arms outstretched, her body pulling her forward. She stops abruptly, right in front of me, and I don't move or breathe. There's doubt in her face—anxiety. Slowly, she reaches a hand out to touch my cheek, flinching as our skin makes contact. Her fingertips glide cautiously over my stubbly jaw, and her other hand comes up to touch my cheek. My eyes are locked on hers, gauging her hesitation. She runs her fingers over my face, through my hair, like she's inspecting for authenticity. I try not to laugh—or cry. Finally, as if the strength has gone out of her, she sinks to the window seat, facing me. Her fingers glide from the back of my neck, under my chin, up to my lips.

"It's you," she says.

I pull her to me, and she grabs my arms, my shoulders, as if she can't hang on. Our lips come together, anxious and hungry. Her mouth is warm and soft, and everything I remember; her scent is intoxicating, like the first day of spring. Her fingers wander to stroke the nape of my neck, making me shiver the way she always used to. I twist my fingers through her short curls and they are *just* as sexy as they were long. I slide my hand to her waist, find her skin, and it's so warm and smooth I want to bury myself in it. We kiss like we're trying to devour each other, and it's the single most electrifying sensation I've felt in my whole life.

We stop to catch our breath, but that only means holding each other so close, we're practically one. I trace the arch of her brow with kisses, and she gasps just the way she always used to. She rests her head on my shoulder, and I close my eyes, breathing in this moment to make it last forever. Her arms are tight around me, but she suddenly goes still. I can feel her heartbeat. But then she starts to shake.

I pull back, peeling myself away enough to see she's crying.

"Oh . . . no," I say, wiping her cheek with my thumb. "It's okay."

She lets out a stuffy sob and shakes her head.

"I'm so sorry."

I kiss her eyelids, taste her tears.

A sharp moan escapes her lips, and she buries her head in my chest.

Someone pounds on the door.

"Viv? Is everything okay? Open up."

She sits bolt upright, wide-eyed, staring at me like I really *am* a ghost.

"My dad."

"It's okay." I turn in the window. "I'll slip out."

"No!" She lowers her voice with effort. "Don't go—don't leave me again."

I brush a stray tear from her cheek.

Her eyes are wide and panicked.

"Viv, if you don't open the door now—"

I take her face in my hands and press my lips to hers. "I'll come back. I promise."

SEVENTEEN

I WATCH VIV'S DAD PATROLLING THEIR HOME LIKE FORT KNOX FROM across the street. There's no way he'd have believed her if she'd said she wasn't upset once he saw her tear-streaked face. Shortly, the light goes out in her room, and I guess we both have to resign ourselves to waiting.

Tomorrow is nothing after two months of never again.

The corner is quiet when I step back through the green light— the most magical, wonderful, weird light in the world. I take a long look around, making sure of where I am. My eyes come to rest on the shrine wrapped around the wooden pole, and this feeling overtakes me. I pull the sunset photograph down and stare at it. My hands tremble, but when I touch Viv's face in the picture, the emptiness doesn't come. These images have reminded me every day for two months that I would never see her again, but now I just close my eyes and inhale her scent lingering on my skin.

I tear another photo off, then one of the cards, and I can't stop. Red and white ribbons tangle in my fingers, and I pull them down, laughing. A teddy bear falls from its pin to the ground, and I practically giggle—I can barely hold it together. None of this stuff means anything anymore. By the time I finish, the pole is as plain as the old one was before the crash and my sides ache from the unfamiliar joy. There's a pile of cards with bullshit sentiments heaped on the sidewalk with the dead flowers and candles. I scoop it all up, making sure not to miss a shred of insincerity, and grin while I carry it across the street to the bus shelter trash can.

I tuck the photographs under one arm, saving them for myself. They used to make me feel so cut off, like she was frozen in the images forever without me, and I'd forget what she looked like if I didn't have them. I used to think there was only one way I might ever see her again. I tip my head back and stare into the cold, starry sky, wondering if there's someone—some*thing* I should thank. Then I wonder if I'd even be saying it to the right sky.

I hesitate by my mom's car in the driveway. Every light in the house is on, even though it's barely six o'clock on a Saturday morning. Mom suddenly acting like *a mom*—so not what I need right now. I close my eyes and return to kissing Viv, her lips soft and warm, her eyes so full of life. It's like just thinking of her sets music playing inside me. I shiver with exhilaration. But when I open my eyes, I'm still standing alone by the car.

I walk heavily up the steps and put my key in the lock.

The house reeks of cigarettes. I slam the front door to give a little warning, and brace myself when my mom comes barreling out of the kitchen, her face tired and angry.

"Where have you been?" she demands. "Do you know what time it is?"

I open my mouth to speak, but my jaw just kind of hangs there. It's not like I've never come in late before. What's odd is that she noticed, or made time in her schedule to care. My cheek twitches. I know what comes next—she'll try to play judge and jury. Lawyers love to do that to their kids.

She stops in front of me, hands on her hips. "I came home late, but you weren't here. Why don't you ever answer your cell phone?"

She folds her arms across her chest. Now *I'm* supposed to be the defense. I try to think up a really good courtroom-solid alibi, but the truth is so goddamn awesome. And so unbelievable.

"Mom, I'm sor—"

"I was just about to call your father . . ."

The music playing inside me cuts out. She can't call him. I thought coming home would attract the least attention until I can sneak back to Viv tonight, but if my dad gets involved . . .

"You don't need to do that," I say.

"Camden, where were you tonight?"

Her eyes are bloodshot. Her clothing stinks of Marlboro.

"When did you start smoking again?" I ask.

She hesitates. Her gaze drops to the ground. She tucks a loose hair behind her ear, but her whole hairdo's a mess.

"Are you . . . high or something?" she asks.

My eyebrows shoot up. Her face is so serious I almost burst out laughing, but I control myself because that would look crazy, and crazy would go over worse than wasted right now. I close my eyes, extend my arms, and touch my fingers to my nose a few times like the police make you do if they think you're drunk. Then I put both my arms out for balance and walk a straight line across the room, heel to toe, turn at the end, and come back.

She stands waiting with her arms crossed, obviously unimpressed with my performance. I glance around her at the dead plants, the dust, the holes where stuff is missing everywhere. She looks so tired and alone. For a second, profound sadness breaks through my mood and I wonder when she got this way. Was it before Dad left?

"Cam, what are you doing?"

I hesitate. "This doesn't feel like a place where people live, Mom."

"What?"

I stare at her, letting the whole depressing picture sink in, and suddenly I'm so upset I can't even talk. I walk over to the entertainment center. The shelf on the right side of the TV is full of DVDs; the left side is empty, like Dad scooped half of them off randomly and just kept on going without looking back. I have this horrible moment where I think I know how he felt—and I hate her for that. I pull some movies down and spread them out evenly across the shelves. Next is the big blank spot over the fireplace. A winter landscape painting used to fill that space. There's a framed poster from a Picasso exhibit hanging in a dim corner. I grab it off the wall.

"What are you doing?" Her face has morphed from pinched and worried to red and upset.

"What we should have done right after he left," I say.

"Stop this—"

I elbow past her on angry adrenaline. How can things be so *right* on one side of a weird green light, and still so fucked up here? I reach the hearth and scrape the poster along the wall until its wire snags the old nail stuck in the plaster. I stand back. The *Blue Nude* looks good above the mantel.

"Did you talk to your father?" she asks sharply. "Was all of this his idea?"

I glare at her. "Was it his idea to let this place become a dump?"

I move to the kitchen and cringe, seeing the mess and grime the way Nina must have. Was the *other* me's house like this? I seriously doubt it. I open the cabinets, spreading the few clean dishes around to fill the half-empty shelves. I hear Mom come in behind me, but I refuse to look at her. I pull the overflowing trash bag out of the kitchen can and toss it outside. Then I turn on the water and start washing every plate, glass, and pan piled up in the sink. She gets quiet. There's only the sound of glasses clinking in the water.

"She was so beautiful, baby. . . ."

Steam rises from the tap running in front of me. I shut off the water.

Mom holds a lit cigarette in one hand, ash accumulating at the end. I'd set Viv's pictures from the shrine down on the counter, and now they're spread out everywhere in front of her. A tear runs down her cheek. She's running her hands over a shot from a biology field trip we took right before I broke my leg. In it, Viv leans toward a bush full of pink flowers, staring down a butterfly. She's got this half smile creeping over her face, waiting for the thing to notice her and take off. She liked doing things like that, finding the exact moment when close became *too* close. I fight an instinct of grief, but then I remember holding her today.

Mom looks up and surveys the less cluttered, if still filthy kitchen.

"When I didn't know where you were, I called Dr. Summers. She wants to help—"

"She *has* helped me," I say. "But I'm starting to think . . . I want to take a little break."

She sets her cigarette down in an overflowing ashtray and looks at me.

"Your coach called."

"Reed?" I exhale impatiently. "He's not my coach."

"He's your vice principal. He's worried about you, sweetie— we all are." She looks around uncertainly at the neatened kitchen and her shoulders slump. "You've had to go through such hell these past few months."

I watch the smoke curl up from her cigarette. This is Mom's idea of parenting—making sure I know how worried everyone is. For a second, I really want to tell her. You can all stop worrying—*I have her back*. But since I can't say that, it's less hassle if I play along.

I sink into the chair next to her.

"It's . . . been hard."

She takes my hand. "I'll get you anything you need to make it easier. Just tell me . . ."

I blink. She just said she'd do anything to make things easier. If I'm going to be with Viv, I need as few people breathing down my neck as possible.

"We can't live this way anymore, Mom."

She stares a long time at her cigarette, but doesn't let go of my hand.

"I know."

"I think . . ." I pull back so I can look her in the eye. "I just need a little space. . . . I *really* want to take a break from therapy."

The worry reenters her eyes.

"Why?"

My gaze falls to the pictures scattered over the counter and my pulse picks up. I can't get used to looking at them in this new way, where Viv isn't gone. I feel like I've been shot out of a cannon. I start collecting them in a neat pile.

"All Dr. Summers wants to do is talk about the past. I have to start looking forward . . ." Viv's face in the top picture makes my heart leap again. How could I even *pretend* to grieve when she's alive? I gesture around the house. "I mean, look at us, Mom. Maybe we both should."

The first rays of sunrise have started to brighten the kitchen.

"This is a different attitude," she says, shaking her head. She takes a final drag or two off her cigarette and mashes the butt into a pile of others. She lifts her face and studies me more calmly than she has in months. My skin feels clammy.

She *can't* say no. . . .

"I need to speak to your dad," she mutters. I cringe, but don't say anything. She's said stuff like that before. "We'll talk more about this later."

She slips off her stool and wraps me in a big, lingering hug. My arms come up automatically to hug her back. I pan over her shoulder at the half-clean kitchen. Anyone who walks in here would clearly see this family has problems. But when I study it more closely, I realize it looks different now. At first I think something's missing by the fridge, until I remember it was the piled-up trash. I spilled water on the floor by the sink, and the white of the tile is showing through the grime. There are still more dishes in the sink than are clean, but I let myself think— this almost looks promising.

EIGHTEEN

IT'S BARELY DARK WHEN I REACH VIV'S HOUSE AGAIN THAT EVENING, but I couldn't force myself to wait any longer than necessary. There's no light in her window when I cross the expanse of lawn, but that doesn't mean anything. All I have to do is knock the right—

"Psssst!"

I halt in front of the weeping willow tree and listen. The air is heavy with silence.

"H—hello?" I whisper.

My eyes aren't fully adjusted to the dark, so I startle when the hanging branches part before me like a curtain.

"You came back," Viv says.

I drink her in slowly, letting my gaze come to rest on her deep brown eyes.

"I told you I would."

She's so like an apparition, I want to reach out and touch her again for reassurance. But I hesitate. The dark curls that frame her face instead of tumbling around her shoulders remind me—I must look different to her, too. I recall the big, confident, grinning guy in the yearbook, and wonder if there's any resemblance of him left in me. I've probably lost thirty pounds since I played, but it's not just the weight . . . he had something else. The look in his eyes isn't one I've been able to find in the mirror. He was clearly a winner, and I'm—

I run a nervous hand through my hair, wishing I'd cut it recently. Maybe she *will* think I'm back from the dead.

I step under the canopy with her. The willow fronds fall almost to the ground, and it's even darker beneath them. Viv steps aside to let me in, her movements slightly jumpy. She backs into the trunk of the tree and stares at me, her breathing shallow and uneven.

"Are you nervous?" I ask.

"No—" she says too quickly.

I reach a hand out to her.

"It's okay."

She hesitates.

I tilt my head. This isn't the reaction she had last night.

"Viv, it's *me*," I say. "What are you afraid of?"

She holds on to the tree like it's some sort of shield.

"Why are you really here? Have you come back to haunt me?"

Oh God, I *am* the undead boyfriend.

"No—no way, Viv, I'm not a ghost." I reach for her again. She

136

starts to pull back, but I twine my fingers through hers, and lean in. "I feel real, don't I?"

Her lips are inches from my own. Our pulses beat a rhythm through the air. Her hand relaxes in mine, though we're both still holding our breath. She closes her eyes and gasps when our lips meet. I press her body between me and the tree, memorizing her with my mouth. Our clothes seem bulky and in the way, suddenly. I open my eyes for a second, just to get a peek at her face. Her long lashes brush her cheek, fluttering the way they always did when she was scared.

I pull away.

She takes a second to let go, but her hands are shaky.

"This is wrong," I say. "I need you to know who I am."

She bites her lip, but it isn't cute. She's afraid.

"You're . . . my Cam."

I exhale. "I'm *not* your Cam. I told you, I'm not a ghost, Viv."

"Well, of course not, but . . ." Her voice trails off.

Gently, I take her hand and place it over my heart.

"I'm alive, flesh and blood."

I wish I'd thought how to explain this earlier, but I'll have to improvise. She has to know—I need her to know.

I'm not *him*.

"I'm not from here. I mean, I come from a place exactly like this, only *you* died there."

Her hand pushes slightly against my chest, holding me at arm's length. I keep one hand over hers and do my best to fill her in while keeping things as simple as possible. I tell her about the accident, about coming through the green light, and finding *her*. I don't mention Nina. I tell her about the differences between our worlds—how everything is so much the same, and yet different. By the time I get through my last fumbling explanation, we're both sitting beneath the tree.

"Two worlds?" she says. "How does something like that even happen?"

I shrug, thinking over the impossibility of it for the hundredth time.

"Maybe there's more than two," I say. "It's like this window just opened up between ours."

She wrinkles her brow. "Why, do you think?"

"I don't know. We both died in the same place . . ." The thought clicks in the back of my mind with something Nina said: *Two months ago—Sunday the fifth*. I sit forward. "If it happened in the same place, on the same day, at about the same time in both worlds—maybe that did something. Maybe *we* did something."

"Like what?"

I shrug. "Maybe our grief, like, tore something open?"

I feel a change in the way she looks at me, but I stare down at my hands. She can't have *him* back, after all. I can't bring myself to face the disappointment in her eyes.

"So . . . *you* lost *me* in your world?" she says. "And you miss her as much as I miss him?"

"Yes—" I latch on to her words and blurt out, "I just thought since we missed each other so much, maybe this is the universe's weird way of making things right."

138

She takes my hands, startling me, then reaches up and brushes my too-long hair out of my eyes. Exactly the way she did at the hospital years ago, in another world. I look up to see her flashing a gorgeous, unfamiliar beauty-queen smile.

"I don't *care* how it happened, Cam. I just can't believe I have you back."

Her lips linger warm and soft on mine until she sighs peacefully and lays her head in my lap. I lean against the tree trunk, afraid to move. I just run my fingers through her curls, listen to her breathing, and ask myself if any of this is real.

"What are you thinking about?" I say after a while. She's quiet, but I've always been able to tell when Viv's mind is busy.

She tilts her face up, and there's a mixture of content curiosity in her eyes that startles me. She looks so much like—herself.

"Tell me more, about how things are different where you come from."

"Oh, I don't know . . ." I shift, comparing myself to Cam the big comeback football star in my head. I decide to focus on her. "You weren't a cheerleader—well, you were, until you quit."

"I did?" She sits up. "How come?"

"Uh . . ." I swallow. How can I explain without her realizing I'm a loser? "Well, you know, I hurt my leg pretty bad, and um— you quit to show your support."

She looks at me, confused. "But why would I do that? You recovered."

I stretch my leg out and touch my knee.

"It didn't happen that way for me."

A heavy silence settles over us, but then she places her hand over mine, on my thigh.

"You quit the team?" she says.

"I didn't need football when I had you." I touch her face with my other hand, tracing the arch of her eyebrow with my thumb. "You—*she* used to always say this thing, 'Who needs them when we have each other?'"

Viv looks puzzled for a second, but nods slowly, and I wonder if she'll accept her own words when things played out so differently here. A subtle grin creeps across her face. She leans in, her lips fast and tender against mine. Her hand slides up my leg, and suddenly my pants feel very confining.

"I *did* used to say that!"

I let out a long breath and lose myself to the impossible tingle of her fingers, her hair, and her intoxicating scent.

"I love your world," she says into my skin.

I laugh in surprise. "Viv, after we both quit . . . we weren't very popular."

"Who needs popular if we have each other?"

Her words stir something inside me I thought had been long dead. I pull her to me and roll on top of her, careful not to crush any precious part of her. She gazes up at me, a familiar, devilish look in her eye.

"*Your* world is better," I counter. "I never want to go home."

A strange look flashes through her eyes. She seems uncomfortable, and I roll gently to one side, propping up on my elbow so I still see her face.

"Why?" she asks.

I hesitate, but right now there's one big difference between this world and mine.

"Because you're here—that's all the reason I need."

Viv doesn't say anything at first, and I start to worry I might have said something wrong. But then she reaches out cautiously, running her fingers lightly up and down my forearm. Her touch grows more confident with each pass.

"Well, that seems unfair," she says, with a hint of mischief.

I relax at her playful tone and nuzzle her hair. "What's unfair?"

"How do *I* know this world is better if I haven't seen yours?"

I'm lost in her silky curls. "You're not missing anything."

"Take me there," she says.

"Where?"

"Where you come from—I want to see it. I want to know it's real."

I pull myself up, hover over her. "You want to go . . . to my world?"

"Let's go now."

"Now?"

She sits up on her knees. "Yeah, we'll see whose world is better. Let's do it right now!"

"But—when did it become a competition?" I mumble, trying to keep up.

My mind spins, unsure what to do. This doesn't seem like a good idea, but wasn't I just as curious about everything on this side? Of course she'd want to see something like that for herself.

My Viv was always impulsive—and when I catch the sparkle in her eyes now, a warm glow begins to kindle inside my chest. It's the same look she had when she suggested we go backpacking in the wild that last weekend we had together. We didn't know what we were doing—she knew setting off alone like that was reckless. But it was an adventure, too, something spontaneous and exciting. She wanted to prove we could do it—or that she could, at least. I stare into those familiar dark eyes and the glow heats up and consumes me. This *is* my Viv.

"Please?" she begs. "It's not fair that you get to come here, but I can't see what it's like there. I'm curious."

"It's really all the same. . . ."

She throws her arms around my neck.

"Please?"

I close my eyes, but I can't avoid the liquid silk of her voice. It will make me ache forever. I have a fleeting thought of Nina. . . . I have no doubt she'd deem this a bad idea. But she's not here. I sigh heavily, as I've done many times before when giving in to Viv, but as soon as the breath escapes my lips, everything feels right *because* it's so routine. I missed even this. From that moment on, it takes effort to keep from grinning, to keep up the bluff that I'm anything less than thrilled.

"Okay, but you'll be bored."

She claps, remembers herself, and covers her mouth. I pull her to a standing position.

"We have to be careful, though, no one can see you because—"

"Oh, right." She smiles. "I'm dead."

She tiptoes to her open window. None of the outdoor lights are on tonight. She climbs inside, and I can hear her rummaging around in the dark. When she drops the few feet back to the ground, she's exchanged her red and white Rams jacket for a thick black sweater. She's tied a silk scarf over her hair and sports dark sunglasses. The combination makes her look like an old Hollywood starlet.

I pull the shades down her nose. "Sunglasses? At night?"

She slides them up into place and throws her head back.

"No one will ever know it's me."

I raise an eyebrow. This ensemble would seem *very* Viv to anyone who knew her, but I don't argue. I'm not planning to run into anyone tonight.

"Fine, I'll save them for later." She pulls them off, tucks them into her pocket, and loops her arm through mine. "Now show me this green-light thing."

I smile and squeeze her hand. I don't like when we're not touching—I want to be reminded every moment that she's with me.

"*This* is where it is?" Viv asks.

"Yeah, you can't see it till you touch it. . . ."

I slide my fingers through the air on one side of the utility pole to just the right spot . . .

"Right there?"

I glance up at her panicked tone. She's standing next to me, arms wrapped tightly around her waist. Her eyes are wild, her face is ashen. She looks like she's going to be sick.

"Are you all right?" I take her by the shoulders, touch her cheek. Her skin is clammy.

Her eyes dart from the pole to the bushes to the sidewalk, but I hold her steady and she eventually focuses on me. Her breathing calms. Some color returns to her face in the pale street light.

"I'll take you home," I say.

She grabs my sleeve.

"No, I'm—" She pauses. "It's just where you . . ."

"It's where we both died," I say, taking her hand again. I gently rub her fingers to warm them. "But that doesn't matter anymore— we're both here now."

She nods her head mechanically and clings to my arm.

"Are you sure you want to do this?" I ask. "There's really nothing to see."

She straightens. "Yes."

I fish around in the air again, and we watch it turn green as my fingers catch the right spot.

"Oh." She reaches out too, but hesitates. "Is it . . . safe?"

"Don't worry, I won't let anything happen to you."

I step into the glow first, not letting go of her hand. Once I'm totally immersed in prickling light, I turn back to help her through.

"You're *green*!" she says, horrified.

"Just close your eyes," I say quickly. "It tingles a little, but I'll get you through fast."

She squeezes my hand hard, but she does close her eyes. I back swiftly out of the light on the other side, pulling her with me as if we were dancing. She stumbles coming through, but I catch her in my arms. She gasps and opens her eyes.

"Oh my God, that was—" She looks around, at the school, the bushes, the traffic light. "We didn't go anywhere."

I smile, lift her chin, and kiss her.

"I told you, everything's the same. It's totally boring—except now *you're* here."

"Am I supposed to just believe you? I want to see what's different!"

"Well, there's the art-room window," I say, gesturing across the lawn to the school. "It's not boarded up on your side."

She raises one eyebrow, but doesn't actually *say* that's completely lame.

"Um, okay, let me think . . ."

I try to come up with something that might satisfy her. Mom could have our house staked out for all I know. I don't own a yearbook, not that we'd be in it. And besides, it's hard to show someone intangible things like who they're *not* friends with and things they *didn't* do in another world. I get anxious just thinking about that. We could go to her house, but that might be awful, and I won't risk running into her parents. Everything that comes to mind is so depressing.

"I know! Take me to my *grave*," she says.

I shudder—that's grotesque. My skin breaks out in goosebumps just from the realization that there's a grave with my name on it back through that green light.

"No," I say.

"Oh, come on, please? How else am I supposed to believe I'm dead?" A look of doubt comes into her eyes. "What if I'm going crazy?"

I sigh. I know that feeling too well. "Can't you just trust me?"

She gets quiet.

"I don't know, what if you came back to me for some other reason?"

I smooth the hair back from her forehead. "What other reason?"

Her voice goes flat and a stricken look crosses her face. "Maybe the universe is messing with me—for the bad things I've done."

"Bad things?" I lift her chin so she has to look me in the eyes. "Like sneaking out to fool around with me?"

"Maybe." She manages a small smile. "Can't fool around till I see what I want to see . . ."

"But it's a graveyard."

"It's just a place. It doesn't mean anything." She touches her forehead to mine. "And I'm alive, right here."

She smothers the objections on my lips in a long, deep kiss. My heart skips, and I can't think. Maybe she's right; it's just a place.

"Fine. We can look at it," I say. "It's just kind of a depressing place."

She pulls me down the street, in the direction of the cemetery. "How depressing can it be to visit my grave—*with me*?"

There's nothing as eerily quiet and spooky as a cemetery in the middle of the night. I haven't been back since the day of her funeral. I just never felt like she was there, not the way I felt her at the corner. Maybe now I know why.

I get us lost a couple of times, but the place isn't that big, and eventually I find the right row of Haywards. You could almost miss the headstone. It's just a small rock with a plaque, but it's the only plot that was dug recently.

"It's that one, over there," I say, pointing.

Viv pulls on my arm. "Come on, then."

I shake my head. "Go ahead."

She tilts her head. "You're not seriously going to make me look at my own grave alone. . . ."

I glance at the rectangular patch of dirt over her shoulder. Grass is just starting to grow over it, sealing her in as if she'd always been there. I shiver.

Viv blots out the scene and touches my cheek. "I'm here with you, Cam—*alive*."

I slip my hand into hers and squeeze. She's taking all of this in such stride; I wish I was half as strong. We approach the plot together. This is actually the first time I've seen the headstone. It wasn't in place during the funeral. There isn't much to it, just her full name—Vivian Frances Hayward—her date of birth, and death.

Without warning, memories from the accident flood my mind—road, rain, squealing tires, the lighter. Everything flashes before me again like it's happening *now*. I close my eyes and shudder as the car impacts the pole, then I climb out to see the shattered window, the blood—and I fall back into the bushes. When I open my eyes again, I'm trembling, clutching Viv to me, burying my face in her neck. She whispers soothing words into my ear, strokes my hair, and now I can hear she's crying too.

I run my hand gently up and down her back while she lays little kisses on my cheek.

"I'm sorry," she whispers. "I'm so sorry, Cam."

I shake my head. "No, I am."

We move away from the lifeless stone in the ground, wandering until we find a wooden bench along a path. I take a deep, cold breath of air.

"I didn't know it would be that way," I say, holding my head in my hands. Even with her beside me, she's still there in the ground too. "We shouldn't have come here."

She doesn't answer, and I look up to see her sniffles have turned into big, silent tears. My stomach sinks. When Viv starts to lose it, there's not much you can do. Every horrible memory of my own disappears. I pull her into my lap and rock her gently while she gasps for breath and shakes with sobs.

"What is it?" I whisper. "You can tell me."

She shakes her head vigorously and says, "I couldn't believe when I lost you, and—it just happened, and—*how could you?*"

"Oh, Viv—I didn't—I would never on purpose . . ."

I rub her back while she sobs into me, and I feel so helpless. All I can do is hold her and listen to her cry. Finally, she seems to gain control over her breathing. She sniffs, and speaks in a shaky voice. "You were just *gone*, and I couldn't bear—"

"Shhh," I whisper, pulling her scarf off to stroke her hair. "It's not your fault."

She makes a sad little whimper and rests her head on my shoulder, holding on to me tightly. Eventually she goes quiet and our breathing falls into sync.

"You said—you *promise*—you'll never leave me again?" she asks.

For a morbid second, I think of the guy in the grave in her world, and how I'm no kind of replacement for him.

"As long as you think you want me," I say.

She clutches me through my jacket, like being in my arms isn't enough. "I'll be better this time too, I promise. . . ."

I close my eyes, inhaling her scent as we kiss. "We both will."

NINETEEN

"CAN'T WE STAY HERE?" VIV ASKS.

I grope around the utility pole, eyeing the lightening sky.

"We can come back all you want, at night," I tell her. "I just don't want to risk someone spotting us."

I frown and continue searching the air. I could swear the spot was right about—my fingers tingle in the right place at last. I don't know why it's so hard to find. I look back into Viv's tear-stained face. Now she looks apprehensive.

"You ready?" I say. "Want to close your eyes again?"

She twists the hem of her sweater.

"What if . . . I don't want to go home?"

I hesitate, unsure if she's serious. "I can't exactly take you to my house and hide you in my closet."

She makes a face, but doesn't say anything, doesn't move. I frown and lift her chin.

"We can go out again tomorrow. I promise."

She eyes the spot where I hold my hand, transparent green, and sighs.

"You go first."

I take her hand and step into the electric air in front of me, turning the space bright green. I have to scrunch my shoulders to fit through. I step clear of the green light on the other side, turning to help Viv the rest of the way, when I see a figure standing on the sidewalk, watching us pass through. I panic, turn back, but I can't warn Viv—she's right behind me. I look around for somewhere to hide, but there's nothing but knee-high bushes and the pole.

"Cam?"

My brain is still shedding the buzz of electricity, but when I recognize Nina's voice, I sigh with relief. Viv steps through, one foot materializing out of the green light, and then the other. She's still holding my hand, and when she's all the way clear, she squeezes hard and gasps.

"That was kind of cool this time!"

With Viv safely through, I exhale and let go of her hand.

"Nina, thank God it's you," I say.

Her eyes flit from me over to Viv and she stiffens. "What are *you* doing here?"

I start toward her, but Viv tugs me back.

"It's okay," I tell her. "Nina already knows everything."

Viv's grip tightens on my left arm. "Oh?"

"I was um . . . showing Viv how it works." I gesture to the utility pole.

Nina hasn't moved. She's wearing a light jacket and tight jeans. Her hair is down—she never pulls it back like at the diner. She stands with her arms at her sides, curling and uncurling the fingers of one hand. I still feel bad for what I said to her about the note in her yearbook, but for some reason I feel even weirder talking to her with Viv on my arm. The way they're staring at each other, they're like opponents at the line of scrimmage.

Nina shakes her head slowly, but her eyes never leave Viv.

"It's not safe for you to be with her, Cam."

I straighten, glancing hastily around. "We haven't been seen."

"What are you doing here again?" Viv says through her teeth.

Nina stares at her about five seconds longer than is comfortable. Then she looks me dead in the eye. "This is dangerous."

"We know what we're doing," Viv says, stepping in front of me. "And it doesn't have anything to do with *you*."

Nina purses her lips. "Do you understand what could happen if either of you are seen?"

"Perfectly," Viv says. "But it still doesn't involve you."

Nina looks to me questioningly. I wonder what the other me might have done. I edge closer to Viv and take her arm. Nina's eyes widen. She sets her jaw, then turns on her heel and walks away. I move to go after her, totally confused, but Viv squeezes my hand *hard*. I wince and pull back, but before I can say anything, she starts off in the opposite direction.

"Viv, wait up—"

I chase after her down the sidewalk. When I touch her arm, she stops abruptly. Her eyes are hurt.

"What's wrong?" I ask. "What just happened?"

"Why does *she* already know you're alive?"

I open my mouth, but nothing comes out. I close it again. Viv crosses her arms, waiting unhappily. What did I get myself into?

"It's kind of a long story—"

"Did you go see her before me?"

I think about Nina standing in the ghostly green light that first night, then showing up at my front door. When was that? Last week? It feels like months ago.

"Nina came to *me*—I didn't even know who she was. I didn't know you were alive."

She narrows her eyes. "What do you mean?"

I eye the pink sunrise to the east. "There's no Nina where I come from. Well, there is, but I've never really met her. . . ."

"You didn't know her?"

I shake my head, holding my palms up. "I'm not sure I would've found you without her."

She plays with her silk scarf, and takes off walking again. I follow. I can't keep up with this.

"What was that about back there?" I ask.

She's gliding again with her usual long stride. The sun breaks over the horizon and she pulls her sunglasses out.

"She was just obsessed with you when you were alive," she says.

I trip over a ridge in the sidewalk. "Huh?"

"She was almost as upset as me when you died. I felt sorry for her. . . . I still do."

"But . . . I thought Nina and I were good friends?"

She makes a face and tucks her hair behind her ears.

"She was in love with you for a while. She didn't take it very well when you told her you just wanted to be friends—'cause you were with *me*, of course. Anyway, she got a little scary—showing up out of nowhere, trying to be seen with you in public, leaving you notes—a little too *stalker* . . . "

My leg starts to ache and I have to slow down. Viv adjusts her pace to match mine.

"Stalker? Nina's not a stalker."

"But if she helped you find me, maybe she's finally over it."

My head has gone into a full spin. It feels too late to tell her that Nina *didn't* point me in her direction on purpose, so I don't say anything. We're back on the sidewalk in front of her house, which is still dark inside and out, though the sun is climbing fast into the sky.

"I guess I better go . . . before I'm recognized," I say.

She grabs my jacket and pulls me close.

"But you'll come back? For me?"

"Of course I will."

A thin line forms between her eyebrows. "Will you be going to see Nina?"

"I . . . don't know," I say. "Would it be bad if I did?"

She drapes her arms around my neck and coos into my ear. "I just couldn't bear it if she stole you away from me."

I go still. Viv's sweet smile makes me think she's unaware of the sting in her words. But after all we've been through—what would make her even say that? I slip my arms around her waist and lean in, erasing the words from her lips.

TWENTY

I SPEND THE WHOLE DAY SUNDAY CLEANING MY ROOM. I HAVE PLANS to sneak Viv over at the first opportunity, and I don't want her to know what a total slob I've been. I clear a ton of crap from under the bed and out of my desk. Assignments from last year that I never handed in, old prescriptions, a couple dishes containing what possibly used to be food. I move on to the closet, only pausing when I run across the white football jersey with the big red number five. I throw it in the garbage can at first, but then I pull it out again. The first time I saw PIKE on the back of a Fowler Rams jersey was when Mike and I had just picked up our JV uniforms together. The printer had spelled *Liu* wrong, and we laughed all the way home about how the hell anyone could screw up a name with only three letters. I run my fingers over the stitching. I know it's too late to make a comeback, despite anything Logan says, but I did have some good times when I wore the uniform.

I fold it up and put it in my dresser drawer.

Viv and I made plans for another blissful night together. She insists on coming through to my side of things again, and though Mom announces she's home for the night, I slip out an hour later. I smuggle some blankets along and take Viv to the elementary-school playground where we fly back and forth on the swing sets until our noses go numb from cold. There's this wooden castle-turret structure with slides twisting down from it, and we climb up inside where I stashed the blankets, and huddle in there together trying to keep each other warm.

"I want to stay here forever," Viv says to me.

"It's a little chilly," I say, pulling the blankets tighter around us.

"Not here in the playground, I mean *here*, in your world."

"Why would you want to stay here?" I let my fingers twist into her curls. "You have everything at home. Your parents, cheerleading—"

"But here I'm so *free*," she says.

"Don't be silly, what do you have to worry about there?"

"Well, I don't need cheerleading!" She hesitates. "You said I gave it up to be with you here—obviously I was on to something."

I look up at the stars through shapes cut out of the roof and remember how happy she used to look in her uniform, beaming at the crowd from the field.

"I always thought you missed it."

"Ugh." She curls her lip. "I can't believe I've kept it up since the accident—well, my parents thought it would be better for me if I did."

I hadn't thought of that. Viv could be having as much trouble dealing with her parents as I'm having with mine. I get stuck with therapy, she still has to cheer.

"Are they the reason you want to leave?" I ask.

She's quiet for half a minute, staring somewhere far away. Then she sits up and gazes deep into my eyes, tracing her finger over the stubble sprinkling my chin.

"It doesn't matter why I want to leave. *You're* the reason I want to stay."

She leans in, and the night is so cold, our eyes pop open when our chilled lips meet. We both laugh. I pull her close and hold her, listening to her breath moving in and out with mine. She's right, none of it matters when you already have the impossible.

"Where do you think we should go after we graduate?" I ask instead. "Find somewhere no one will recognize us?"

"Ooh, Tahiti—*your* Tahiti!" Viv says, and shivers. "Let's go somewhere far away and eternally warm."

I stare at her, surprised. "I thought you never wanted to see another beach after that trip to Hawaii with your cousins."

"Hawaii?" she asks. "I've never been. I think I'd remember a trip to island paradise."

I shake my head, confused. "Sophomore year? You went for spring break when your cousin Amanda got into Harvard. You came home with such a bad sunburn, you swore you never wanted to see another palm tree again."

Viv's face goes gray. "Harvard?"

"Yeah. She's still there—premed."

She frowns. "Amanda's on her second stint at a treatment facility."

We both shift uncomfortably. The way I understood it, Viv's cousin overcame a budding drug problem on her *way* to Harvard, but I'm afraid to say anything more.

"She *could* have been brilliant." Viv sniffs. "Guess she handled the pressure better here. More points for your world."

I cough in surprise. Viv always admired Amanda, even when she saw her struggle. It's strange listening to her write her off now.

"Well, Tahiti's a little far, anyway," I say, changing the subject. "What if you wanted to visit home?"

She waves her hand dismissively. "I'll send a postcard. How much postage do you think I'll need to send it through the green light?"

I laugh, and we both shiver and cuddle up closer.

"We don't *have* to wait till then," Viv says after a little while.

"If you want to stay in my world, we do. My mom *will* find me and kill me if I stay in the same dimension as her and don't graduate."

She laughs and I lift her chin up so she meets my eyes.

"But if we went to your side . . ."

She shakes her head vigorously. "No way."

I roll my eyes. She's always been stubborn, and this is clearly becoming something she won't budge on. "When school's over, no one will care what we do," I say. "We can figure out where to go then."

She snuggles closer to me under the blanket, resting her cheek on my chest.

"You mean we can figure out how to both be *here*."

TWENTY-ONE

WHEN I LEAVE FOR SCHOOL MONDAY MORNING, THE HAPPYMAIDS are trooping single-file into my house. Mom actually took a day off work to supervise this. I didn't tell her I thought it'd take more like a week. I have memories of our kitchen floor, and it's white, not gray.

Still, it's nice that she's trying.

I get to the front doors of Fowler High before the bell rings for a change. I forgot how crowded it could be trying to get inside with the rest of the student body. Some freshman carries a poster-board project he constructed over the weekend; a girl I recognize from the smokers' bus stop runs past me for a nic fix. Another girl teetering in front of me in ridiculously high pink heels almost tumbles down the stairs before I reach out and catch her.

"You okay?" I ask, when she's got both stilettos under her again.

"Yeah, thanks, I—Camden?"

I let go of her fast. "You should be more careful in those things, Tash."

I head past her up the stairs, but before I've gone two steps I'm slammed backward into the railing by a very red-faced Logan West.

"You messing with my girl, Pike?"

It's difficult to form a coherent sentence when your back is bent at an unnatural angle over a metal railing.

"Your girl?"

"Don't get any ideas this time, understand?" He nods at her. "That right there is mine."

I glance over at Tash, whose hair is done up so she resembles a poodle in a pink outfit. Even if Viv's kiss wasn't warm on my lips, the suggestion is so ridiculous, I laugh out loud.

"Congrats, I didn't know you were official," I say. "Last I heard, you two were just friends with benefits."

Logan shoves me again, and for a moment I think he's going to throw the punch he's been waiting to deliver since Viv left him, and send me clear over the railing . . . but it still doesn't come. There's a wide receiver standing between me and the not-so-star quarterback.

"Hey, West, why don't you go buy your *girlfriend* practical shoes?" Mike says. "If Pike hadn't caught her, she'd have fallen on her ass."

Logan's face darkens from red to purple. He looks from me to Mike, then down the steps at Tash.

"Girlfriend?" Tash's smile spreads as she looks from Mike to Logan. "I'm texting Niki!"

Logan passes us by, trying to get a word in while Tash effectively broadcasts the news to the whole school.

I glare at Mike.

He raises his eyebrows. "Good morning to you too?"

My mood darkens for the first time in days. I might not be on the team anymore, but when did Mike decide that means I need to be coddled and protected? I think of the Red King, standing proud in front of the school—on Viv's arm. What would she think of Mike fighting my battles for me?

"I can deal with Logan myself," I snap.

"Sorry, were you *trying* to get that nose of yours broken?"

I clench my jaw. "Just let me handle my own shit. Don't you have some of your own to deal with, or are you too nice a guy to get yourself punched?"

"Dude, what the—"

"Just back off, okay?" I start up the stairs, but the look on Mike's face slows me down. How do I explain that I don't want to seem like a loser compared to—another me?

When I get to the top, he calls out, "What the hell happened to you, Pike?"

I shrug and call over my shoulder, "I had a great weekend."

"Mr. Reed!" I call across the hall on my way to lunch.

My ex-coach stops in his tracks and waits for me out of the flow of student traffic.

"Mr. Pike? Is there something I can do for you?"

I feel a little stupid coming to him about this, but now that I'm standing in front of him, I can't exactly back down.

"I was hoping, I mean, I want to ask you . . . Do you think I could get into a P.E. class?"

He starts to open his mouth, but I barrel forward before either of us can think.

"I have second period free, and I mean, I know there's my leg and all, but I just think maybe it would be good for me. I kind of—want to get back in shape. Not to play again, obviously, but I don't know . . ."

My face grows hot. Reed stands there impassively. I swear he doesn't even blink for a whole minute.

"If you think you're up for it . . . I'll have the office take care of it, Camden."

My jaw drops open. I thought he'd at least say he had to think about it.

"Okay. Thanks, um—Coach."

"Cam," he says as I hurry away. "You'll have a locker assigned tomorrow. Bring gym clothes."

I'm *in*.

I pass through the lunchroom, but only to buy food. The burgers haven't improved any since Viv and I picked at them last year, but I heap on a ton of condiments until they appear edible. I rewrap them in foil and ditch my tray by the doors before heading out into the hall. But when I see Mike hunched over his sketchbook in our usual doorway, I slow down.

He nods at the burgers when I approach. "You going back on food?"

"I could put on a pound or two," I say cautiously.

I just want to go find a place to sit—by myself. I steal a glance at the open notebook in his lap, which features a detailed rendition of what appears to be a sexy girl wildebeest thing. I raise an eyebrow. New territory for him.

"So, you going to eat standing up, or what?" he says.

He's just sitting there chewing his energy bars and drawing, as usual, like I wasn't a total ass to him this morning. I hover a few long seconds and sit down.

I chew my food mechanically, trying to make every bite last so I have an excuse not to talk. I watch things going on around us instead. Keisha Todd and James Clark are making out across the hall. The Math Club guys next to us are hunched over notebooks doing equation drills. At one point, I see Tash Clemons and her posse click down the hall—apparently they *coordinated* wearing stilettos so they could hang on to one another to walk all day.

"So I was just curious," Mike says, sticking his pencil behind his ear. "I saw the memorial is gone . . . did *you* take it down?"

Why can't he just not want to talk to me after this morning, like any normal person would?

"Yeah," I say, wiping mustard from my mouth.

"Mind if I ask why?"

"*You're* the one who suggested I get on living my life. What do you want?"

"No, I—well, maybe I did." He grips his power-drink bottle.

"I mean, do what you need to. I just wondered what it means."

"It means I took it down." I crumple my wrappers.

"It's just bizarre," he says. "One day you're slumped over on the floor after Logan looks at you, the next you're helping Tash out and looking for a fight. What happened this weekend, Cam?"

I stand up fast and sling my backpack over my arm. "I can't stay sad forever."

TWENTY-TWO

IT'S BARELY DUSK WHEN I GET TO THE CORNER, BUT I'M SICK OF waiting. I never feel quite complete when I'm not with Viv. After ducking through the green light, I immediately head in the direction of her house. There are clouds in the sky, but it's not cold enough for it to snow. Still, I pick up my pace to keep from shivering.

I start thinking of places where Viv and I can be alone tonight—somewhere warmer than the playground, maybe even a movie theater. No one would see us in the dark. Chattering voices catch my attention when I'm halfway through an intersection, and I look up to see a group of high school kids coming right at me. There are a few guys and a couple girls, but I don't recognize any of them at first glance. They're caught up in some conversation about a TV show, but then one of them glances over at me, and I glance back—and it's *Logan*.

He stops, and I stop, and I'm pretty sure *both* of our hearts stop for a second-long infinity, judging by his face. I've never seen those shifty, calculating eyes get so huge.

"Hey—"

I take off before he can finish the word.

I run through backyards faster than I think I ever ran in football. I yank my hoodie up and jump a fence, avoid a pool, and skip over to the next block. I run up that street until I realize I'm out in the open, and I dash down someone's driveway, behind a garage. A dog barks at me, and I skip to the next yard, but then I start to recognize where I am. I glance back, but no one's directly on my tail, so I head straight through two more yards until I get to Nina's house. I crouch against the siding behind the bushes by her porch, waiting for a posse of five people to come flush me out.

After several minutes of silence, my heart stops pounding quite so hard, and I guess my brain switches out of fight-or-flight mode because my right leg feels like it's on *fire*. I limp out of hiding, but all I see is the empty street. I don't hear anything but a car coasting down the next block. I lean forward, massaging the throbbing muscles over my aching bones, and I exhale. I'm such a goddamn idiot. Why the fuck wasn't I paying attention?

Someone shouts farther down the street and my body goes rigid. The relative feeling of safety abandons me. I reach for the porch railing, and hesitate. The last time I saw Nina, everything was so weird. What will she do if I bang on her door now?

The squeal of tires on asphalt pierces my ears, and my priorities shift—what will happen if I get caught out here? I scramble onto the porch and press the doorbell. A few seconds pass, but I don't hear anyone coming after the chime rings inside the house. I tap on the door frame, turn a nervous circle, and glance out into the darkness. I'm just thankful no one turned on the porch light tonight. I'm about to press the bell again when the door finally swings open and Owen stares up at me.

I nudge him aside, step into the safety of the hall, and turn the deadbolt behind me. I slump against the door and exhale. Owen is still gazing at me mutely.

"Hey, buddy," I say. "How you doing?"

He gives a faint smile, but doesn't say anything.

"Um . . . is Nina around?"

He shrugs. The hair on his forehead is moist with sweat and he's wicked pale.

I kneel in front of him.

"Owen, where's Nina?"

His eyes are glassy and unfocused. I try to remember why Nina said he was sick before . . . diabetes? What do you even do about that? I glance around the house to see if anyone else is around, but it's mostly dark.

"Is she upstairs?" I ask.

"I don't wanna bug her . . ." He trails off.

"C'mon, O." I take his hand. "Let's go see her, okay?"

His fingers are cold in mine. He trips on the stairs, but I catch him and try to keep my cool. Something's seriously wrong with the kid. Nina's door is closed when we get to the hallway. I knock, but when she doesn't immediately answer, I open up and go in.

She's curled on her bed, which is as neatly made as the last time I was in here. She's dressed in jeans and a sweater, her eyes closed. There's a notebook open in front of her where she's scribbled a few math problems, but she's fallen asleep with a graphic novel in one hand. Her iPod lies by her side, but her earbuds have fallen out, and it's so quiet, whatever playlist she was listening to must have ended. I grab her calf and shake her.

"Nina!"

She kicks out and shrieks, but I dodge her foot. She flies back against her pillows, getting tangled in her earbuds.

"Jesus—*Cam!?*"

"Something's wrong with Owen," I say.

"What the hell are you—" Her eyes fly to her brother. "What— Owen?"

She takes one look at him swaying by my side, and she's off the bed like a shot, feeling his forehead and talking to him.

"O, what's wrong? What's the matter?"

"I'm hungry," he mumbles.

Nina's eyes get wide. "What time is it? Did you have dinner?"

Owen shakes his head. "Aunt Car said you'd fix something soon."

She grips his shoulders, her jaw tight. "This is important, Owen. Do you remember if she gave you an injection before she left?"

He hesitates for what seems like forever, then he nods.

"Are we going to eat soon?"

Nina's face crumples. She looks around like she's trying to formulate a plan, then she gets up and moves for the door.

"Hey, what can I do?" I ask. "Do we need to call an ambulance?"

"He needs sugar," she yells, already halfway down the hall.

Owen looks like he's about to pass out. I scoop him up in my arms and follow Nina down the stairs. When we reach the kitchen, she digs through the fridge until she pulls out a huge container of orange juice. I place Owen gently in a chair while Nina sloshes juice into a glass. She's almost as pale as her brother. She brings the cup to his lips, but her hand is unsteady. I take it from her and urge him to drink.

"I'm tired," he mutters, turning away from the cup.

"*Drink it*, Owen," Nina pleads.

"Owen, drink the juice, buddy," I say. "I can't tell you all my football secrets if you fall asleep."

He rolls his head toward me and peeks one eye open. I try to keep the anxiety off my face. I nod at him and smile encouragingly. He takes the smallest sip at first, but eventually finishes every drop. Nina seems to calm as I set the empty glass aside, and the tension goes out of my shoulders. I don't know how juice will help him, but this has to be a good sign.

"What are you even doing here?" she asks me, exhausted.

"Nothing . . ." I hesitate, reliving the moment when Logan saw me. It seems like a hundred years ago. She doesn't need to know about that. "But it's a good thing I showed up."

Ten minutes later, Owen is alert, if still feeling crappy. I carry him back up to bed where he can get comfortable, and Nina checks his blood sugar at least fifty times before bringing him peanut butter and jelly for dinner.

"You sure he doesn't need to go to the hospital or anything?" I ask.

Nina shakes her head and rises to stand at the end of his bed. "He'll be okay."

Owen crosses his arms and frowns. "I'm never going to be okay."

"Do you feel worse again?" I ask, eyeing the blood-sugar meter.

He glances at me, but then fixes his eyes on the goal posts dotting his comforter. "I can't play football if I'm sick all the time."

"This wasn't your fault, O," Nina says.

I sit down on the edge of the bed. "People play sports with a lot worse problems. You just have to take care of yourself."

He doesn't look up.

"Football is *not* about being perfect, Owen." I swallow, trying not to think too much about what I'm saying. "The best players are the ones that want it the most, try the hardest." I pick up a football he's got sitting on a shelf, surprised at how good it feels in my hands. He catches it when I pass it to him. "It'd be sad if the Rams never got a quarterback as awesome as you're going to be."

He looks at me skeptically, but the scowl is gone.

"Isn't that right, Nina?"

She doesn't answer. I glance where she'd been standing, but she's gone.

I turn back to Owen.

"You going to be all right for a little while?" I ask.

He lies back and sighs. "Yeah . . . thanks, Cam."

Nina's not in her room, though the door is open. I glance briefly at the picture on the bookcase again. There's no mistaking it now—it's her as a little girl, scrunching her freckles and smiling with her mom, dad, and baby brother. I wonder if Owen was always sick. I wonder how old Nina was when they died.

I find her in the kitchen, wiping orange juice off the counter with a wad of paper towels.

"You okay?" I ask. It's a stupid question.

"I'm fine."

Her eyes are dry, if red-rimmed. She scrubs hard at something I can't see on the counter, but doesn't look up. I move closer, not sure what to say. It seems like Owen was easier to comfort.

"He's going to be okay," I say. "You said so yourself."

"I know." Her voice is short, annoyed.

"Then what's the matter?"

She balls the soggy paper towels up and launches them right past me into the sink.

"He wouldn't have gotten sick at all if I'd been paying better attention!"

"Whoa." I hold up my hands. "Nina, this wasn't your fault."

She makes a dismissive noise and crosses to the sink. I hesitate, trying to find the right words, and put my hand on her shoulder.

"Don't be so hard on yourself," I say. "Taking care of your brother shouldn't be *your* responsibility."

She stands still for a moment when I touch her. Then she pulls out the paper towel mess and starts scrubbing at the sink, avoiding my eyes. I let my hand fall away.

"Thanks, but who else is going to do it? Aunt Car never remembers."

"Well, maybe you should talk to her—*she's* the adult. It's just not fair—"

"Life isn't fair, Cam!" she snaps.

I stare at her.

"There isn't a day I don't wish I could go back to my old school, my old house—where my parents worried instead of me *or* Owen. But when they died, all of that changed." She turns away, letting her hair screen her face. "I guess I can't expect you to understand."

I grit my teeth. Doesn't she remember who she's talking to?

"In case you've forgotten, I have a gimp leg, my dad walked out, and my girlfriend died—"

"And now look, you've got her back," Nina finishes for me.

My jaw drops, but I keep my cool. I can't expect her to understand that the universe owes me and Viv. It's just making things right.

"I still had to live through it."

"This isn't the way things are supposed to work. My parents died, and they're gone forever."

"Look, I'm sorry about your parents. I really wish you could have them back too—"

"People die, Cam." Her tone is icy and calm. She looks me straight in the eye. "As much as I want them back, I've accepted that's never going to happen, and *I'm* the one who has to be here for my brother."

I bite the inside of my cheek.

"Don't blame me just because I happen to be lucky."

"You think this was all meant to be or something?" She snorts. "What's happening with you and Viv—it's dangerous and it's wrong."

I open my mouth to reply, but her words make me hesitate. How can she say it's wrong? It's fucking wonderful! Still, it seems cruel to rub her misfortune in her face. I lower my voice.

"I can't lose her again, Nina."

Her face falls, and now I do feel sorry for her. I'm willing to bet the Nina back home still has both her parents.

"Just . . . be careful, Cam."

"I will." I touch her hand. "I really am sorry. . . ."

She stares down where our fingers overlap, then she pulls away. "I am too."

TWENTY-THREE

VIV ISN'T HOME WHEN I FINALLY MAKE IT TO HER HOUSE. THE window is open, but the light in her room is off. I call softly outside, but there's no response from the shadows or the tree. I circle the house carefully, but the only light I see comes from the den, where her dad has nodded off in front of the TV. The glowing kitchen clock makes me realize I was at Nina's longer than I thought.

She might have gone to look for me, but if I go searching for her we could miss each other completely. I lean against the tree, hidden under the willow branches, and wait for her to come back. The longer I sit alone, the harder it is to fight fatigue. Everything that's happened tonight has been so intense, all I want to do is lie in Viv's arms and listen to the soothing sound of her voice. She might've just gone for a walk . . . but after a while I get this nagging feeling. What if she thinks I just didn't come? What would she do? I remind myself that Viv *has* other friends here. Wouldn't any girl who thinks she's been stood up go cry about it to other girls? Except I can't really see Viv explaining to Tash Clemons how her dead boyfriend didn't show up when he said he would.

The TV light finally goes out. Mr. Hayward is off to bed. I stand up to stretch, exhausted, and sore from sitting on knobby roots. If I had my phone with me, I could try to call her, but I'm not sure my calling plan covers interdimensional roaming. I glance at Viv's darkened window one last time and reluctantly head home, planning all the way to the utility pole how I'll make it up to her tomorrow—how I'll beg forgiveness in tiny kisses all over her body.

My thoughts are somewhere on her upper thigh when a light in front of me grabs my attention. I glance up in time to see Viv stumbling out of the green glow on the corner. She doubles over coughing, and I run to her.

"Viv!" I pull her up straight, holding her close while the energy leaves her body. She's limp at first, but soon her fingers close around mine and she's staring into my eyes.

"Cam?" she asks. "What are—I was looking for you!"

I lean into her. "I'm sorry, I'm here now."

My lips caress hers, but she pulls away. "Where were you?"

I let go of her, and she steps further back.

"I . . . I've been here," I say. "I mean, at your house waiting for you. I thought—"

"You were supposed to come hours ago—I was so worried!" She touches her lips uncertainly. "I thought something might've happened . . ."

"Don't be upset," I say. I want to reach for her, but I'm afraid she'll pull away again. "It was a misunderstanding. I did come earlier, but Nina's brother was sick and—"

"You were with *her*?"

I stop talking, cut by the sharpness of her voice.

"Why would you do that?"

"It's not—I just . . . I was on my way to your house."

She processes my words, and the way it makes me feel is so uncomfortably foreign. Viv has never been jealous before . . . it was one of the things about us. I knew I was all she ever wanted, and she knew I felt exactly the same way about her. But now Viv is clearly jealous of Nina and I don't know how to deal. I wonder if the other me ever had to contend with this.

"Vivee," I say, using a pet name I save for special occasions. "You don't actually think I'd want to see Nina more than *you*?"

Her body stays stiff and closed, but the creases in her forehead smooth. I move close again, prying one of her hands loose.

"Nina's nice, but you're—" I pull her into my arms. "You're *you*."

She resists another second, searching deep in my eyes, but then she relents. Her lips are warm and needy, but the way they meet mine is so achingly familiar. My skin still prickles. I've been waiting for this all night, and with our kiss, I feel we're whole again.

TWENTY-FOUR

"CAM? WHAT ARE YOU DOING IN HERE?"

I glance up from tying my sneaker. "I didn't know you were in this class."

"Um, are *you*?" Mike looks at my T-shirt and sweats, and shoves his bag in a locker. "I thought you got exempt from the gym requirement."

I shut my locker and spin the combination. "I asked to be let in."

"You *asked* for gym class?"

"I'm ready for it again."

"But your—" Mike hesitates, glancing at my right leg. "You *do* know it's Hernandez second period?"

I shrug. Hernandez is uniformly loathed by students—though mostly the girls—for requiring us to actually break a sweat in class. But that's what I'm here for. I start stretching my shoulders.

Mike pulls off his shirt and starts to say something else, but it's muffled. I take one look at him and am relieved I already changed. My flat, pale torso looks sickly compared to someone who regularly lifts weights. I close my locker quietly and slip out to the gym.

Hernandez starts the class off running laps. Everyone groans, but everyone moves. If you don't when he whistles, he fails you for the day. I'm keeping up with the back of the herd, trying to stay focused, when he calls my name.

"Pike, come here."

I jog over.

"I'll exempt you from running. Have a seat till they're done."

I glance at the group already halfway around the gym. There is no way I can sit still now that I've started.

"If it's okay, sir, I'd like to participate."

He glances automatically at my leg, just like Mike did. He may be the soccer coach, but the whole school knows what happened to me. I wore sweat pants on purpose, to cover the scar.

"I was told not to go too hard on you," he grunts.

"I appreciate the concern, but I'd like to at least try."

Hernandez considers this for fifteen whole seconds. "All right, Pike, it's your call." He directs me to the back of the group and barks, "Use it or lose it, people!"

I fall back in with the freshmen struggling to keep up.

When you haven't attended a gym class in over two years, you tend to forget sports like dodge ball even exist. There's an awkward moment after we finish running when I realize teams will be picked, but Hernandez doesn't mess around with high-school hierarchies. He divides the class in half where we stand, and I end up spending most of the period trying to hit Mike for fun. Actually, I get a little annoyed when I realize he's trying *not* to hit me, but plenty of other people are, so I don't make it an issue.

By the time I head back to the locker room, I smell like sweat and basketball rubber, but I feel okay. I won't say *good* yet. My head is heavy with lack of sleep, but my body feels different, like it's starting to wake up. I take a minute after the bell rings to stretch my leg. It does ache, though not in the usual way. It's stiff and weak from the workout, not throbbing with pain. Tomorrow will be harder . . . but I'm almost looking forward to it.

"Cam . . ." Mike comes up just as I'm about to leave for trig. His voice is barely audible under the din of guys shouting and slamming lockers. "I saw your Facebook this morning. What's going on?"

I blink. "Facebook? Huh?"

He glances around and speaks under his breath.

"Don't you think you're taking it a little far?"

The sweaty locker room is too loud and too cold. Dread bubbles up inside me and I have to force my feet to stay where they are and not run straight home to my laptop.

"I haven't been on Facebook," I say slowly. "In months."

Mike just looks at me. "Well, never mind, then. I guess it was a ghost."

My skin goes clammy. It probably *is* Logan this time. That's an easy enough prank for him to pull . . . but I can't bring myself to ask Mike exactly what he saw. I close my locker and it jams; I pull it open again and slam it.

The second hand on the clock in my civics class doesn't tick. It crawls around the dial in one agonizingly slow motion. I tried logging in to Facebook from the library, but the site is blocked. I'd skip the rest of today altogether, but the last thing I need now is to draw more attention. Hopefully anyone who might see it or care is stuck in the school too. I tap my pencil on the edge of my desk and hastily fill in the last four bubbles on my test—A, B, C, D. The bell rings. I bolt out of my seat, get halfway to the door, then have to double back and hand the exam to Mrs. Moore.

I half limp, half run around the corner onto my street. My heart feels like it's going to pound out of my chest, but I have to get to Facebook before Mike sees it again. I spot a figure perched on my front steps in broad daylight. *Viv?* My heart stops. But as I get closer, I realize it's not Viv—it's Nina. I storm up to the house.

"What happened?"

She rises. "What do you *think* happened?"

I drop my keys, pick them up, and fumble to get the right one into the lock. I twist the handle and pull, and at last the door swings open. Nina comes inside on my heels.

"You want to tell me why I went to lunch today only to hear Logan West ranting to the entire cafeteria that he saw you *alive* last night?"

"Oh . . ." I get tangled in the strap of my backpack, trying to throw it down.

"And then Viv ran into the bathroom with her hands over her face, either laughing or crying, and—are you even listening to me?"

I glance over my shoulder, halfway down the hall toward my room.

"I just need to take care of something . . ."

My laptop is open on my desk with my iPod plugged in—except I always leave it closed. I hit the track pad and crash into my chair, but the computer takes its time waking up from sleep mode. I start tearing at my hair, but then the password screen comes up. It takes me three tries to type the password I've had for five years, *RainbowTrout*. But the screen doesn't change except to say INVALID PASSWORD. I clench my teeth and type it again, but it still doesn't work. I dig my fingers into my thighs and suppress a moan . . . but then I think to try Viv's password, *OneAndOnly*.

The browser appears with my Facebook page still up.

"What are you doing in here?" Nina comes in behind me, making me jump. "Did you even hear what I said?"

I squirm in my seat, but with the screen open, we can both see the new message written on my wall:

Love you forever.

Goosebumps rise up on my arms. I glance at Nina. Her mouth is open.

"What *is* that?"

I log in to Viv's account and delete the post quickly. While she was here, she changed both our profile pics to a shot she took months ago on her phone. It's a close-up of us kissing inside her car. She couldn't know how much I hate it, that it reminds me of how she died. I hastily delete it too, leaving both our profile pics empty silhouettes.

"Did anyone see that?" Nina demands.

"Just Mike—I think." I unfriended everyone but Mike and Viv two years ago.

Nina slams the door of my room.

"That's one too many! Did you hear what I said about Logan? Viv can't exist here, Cam, this has got to stop—"

"Yeah, I know, okay?" I stand up and pace across the room. "Just let me deal with this—I'll talk to her."

"You think you can *talk* to her? Are you nuts?"

"She'll listen to me—"

"What about Logan?" she demands. "Viv's not the only one acting stupid."

I rub my hand over my face. "It won't happen again."

"And what if it does, what then?"

"Just—stop!" My voice breaks.

The room is silent except for the hum of my computer processor. Nina doesn't say anything for a while, and I'm hoping she'll just leave, but then she moves toward me. She puts a hand on each of my arms and looks into my face.

"I know it was hard—when she died. But if you leave her now, you'll both just be somewhere else. It doesn't have to be like . . . death."

She's so close I catch the scent of something like peaches in her hair. She slides her hands down into mine and turns her face up. Her eyes are clear, and the way she's leaning toward me—I pull away and let her hands drop.

"I'm not leaving her, Nina."

She steps back and supports herself against the wall by the window.

I sink back into my chair and pick at the edge of my shirt. I'm not sure if it's from gym class, or stressing about Facebook all day, or not getting any sleep . . . but I'm utterly exhausted. I rest my face in my hands.

"I haven't been this tired since the night she died."

Nina sits on the bed and leans toward me. "Don't let her push you around."

I swallow hard. "I don't—she doesn't."

"You know that's not true."

I pick up my iPod and start scrolling through the music. There's a new playlist called "Vibes à la Viv," full of her favorite bubblegum love songs.

"You can survive without her, Cam—you *did*—and so did she."

I glance up at her. Viv and I might have survived, but if I asked I think she'd agree, neither of us was really living. I can't listen to Nina's *life goes on* speeches anymore.

"Okay, look, we'll be more careful," I say.

She grabs a handful of my pillow at her side and shakes her head. "Until the next time, right?"

I plug the iPod into my speakers and hit play. The room fills with synthy, squeaky music. My bedroom door swings open.

"I thought you were here, sweetie. I came home early to—" My mom stops.

"Mrs. Pike—" Nina leaps up and collects herself. "I mean, you must be—Mrs. Pike."

Mom blinks at Nina and shifts her questioning gaze to me. I shut off the music.

"Bye, Nina," I say. "Sorry you have to leave."

Nina makes for the door, but Mom stops her.

"No, wait—" She has this weird, awkward smile on her face. "Nina? Cam doesn't bring many friends by. Would you like to stay for dinner?"

Nina gives me this death-ray glare like everything wrong in the universe right this minute is my fault.

I look at Mom. "You? Cooking dinner?"

Mom's face turns a shade of pink. "I thought we could have

Chinese takeout—at home?"

"Thanks, Mrs. Pike . . . I have to get home to my brother." Nina slides past Mom and smiles. "I love what you've done with the place—" She stops abruptly. "So—let me know if you need help—with that trig homework, Cam."

Nina's out the door before anyone can say another word. Mom blinks at me, confused, but then she gives me this great big encouraging smile and disappears, humming down the hall.

TWENTY-FIVE

WHEN I PUSH THROUGH THE GREEN LIGHT THIS TIME, VIV IS ON the corner waiting for me. I almost get wedged into the narrow portal when I see her sitting on a landscaping rock with her Rams football jacket pulled tight around her.

"Hey, beautiful," I say, greeting her with a kiss. "Didn't I say I'd come pick you up?"

"I thought we could go to your side tonight . . . I didn't want to miss you if you stopped anywhere else on the way."

My gut twists and I think of what Nina said—but Viv is *not* pushing me around—she's just confused. And who can blame her after last night? All she needs is a little reassurance.

I raise my eyebrows. "I have no plans to see Nina tonight."

She gives me a stern look. Then she cracks a smile, throws her arms around my neck, and laughs.

"I've missed you so much since yesterday!"

I smile, relieved. "Your playlist was cute."

"You noticed that?"

"And the Facebook post—" I tense, thinking about it again. I pull back and hold her shoulders at arm's length, trying to give her my most serious stare. "Viv, you can't do stuff like that. . . . If anyone saw that, they'd think *I* did it."

"But you *do* love me forever, don't you?" she asks, running her finger along my jaw.

I give in, pulling her close and grazing her full lips with my own.

"Just don't do it again."

She whispers in my ear. "I loved that I was one of your *only* Facebook friends."

I fight a pang at her words, which is dumb. Viv and I deleted everyone else from our friends' lists on purpose. It was more than just symbolic; we got less shit from all the people who still called themselves Rams. But I think of her on the arm of her football star and wonder how many Facebook friends *he* had. I take her hand and remind myself, *I'm* her Cam now. She still has everything she wants . . . doesn't she?

"Anyway, you can't scold me." She pulls me toward the pole, starts searching the air for the green light, and glances over her shoulder. "I heard you haunted Logan last night."

I pull back. My stomach sinks.

She smirks and straightens. "He was telling anyone who would listen—'I saw Pike's ghost on the street!'—you should've seen the look on his face! Mike got so upset. I had to run to the bathroom so no one would see me laughing my head off!"

I press my palms into my eyes. "I wasn't thinking—that was so stupid."

"Maybe he'll leave me the hell alone for a while."

"What?"

She arches her eyebrow. "He seems to think he's allowed to put his hands all over me lately."

My vision goes red at the thought of Logan doing *anything* to Viv.

She bites her lip. "Without you around, he won't take no for an answer."

"Let's go find him." I ball up my fists. "That asshole has it coming." I tense to take off running, but it's like I can hear Nina's voice warning me about acting stupid. I let my hands fall to my sides and glance around. "But if I get found out . . . I won't be able to come here anymore."

Viv smiles. "Then we'll go to your side."

My head starts to throb. This again. I'm horrified to feel a twinge of annoyance, but she never lets up on the idea that my world is somehow better. It makes no sense.

"Not if you keep breaking into my house and posting stuff where everyone *there* will see you—"

"You're the one who got caught," she says.

"But I wasn't trying to get Logan's attention!"

"I never got noticed at all." She smiles smugly.

I look her in the eye. "Mike saw it."

"Screw Mike," she sneers.

The twinge in my brain starts working its way up to full-on headache. "Why do you want to go to my side so bad anyway?"

"I just like it better," she says, pulling me back to the utility pole and feeling around in the air.

"But why?"

"Things are less complicated there." She holds one transparent green hand in front of her and looks at me seriously. "But also . . . I think I might be jealous."

Without another word, she flashes into the green and disappears. I move my lips soundlessly. All I can do is follow, crouching down through the electrified air until we're both wheezing energy back on my side.

"What's there to be jealous of?" I ask after I catch my breath.

"It's nothing, forget it."

"It obviously means something to you," I say. "Tell me?"

She comes at me for a kiss, but I hold my hand in front of my mouth. She frowns.

"I feel like you loved me more here. I think I'm jealous of . . . myself."

Every reassurance I had ready goes silent on my lips. I take a breath, but I don't know what to say. It takes a long minute for me to even wrap my head around the idea.

Viv is jealous of how much I loved . . . Viv?

We start walking again, down the sidewalk toward the athletic field.

"It was hard being with the school football star," she says. "I loved you so much, but you were *so* big . . . sometimes it didn't feel like there was enough of you left for me."

"But if he was the same as me—how could he have loved you *less*?"

"I'm sure he didn't," she whispers. "But what I—*she*—had here . . . you were devoted to her; she had you all to herself."

I stare through the chain-link fence across the cold, dark grass. I thought she was worried about Nina, but she wants what her dead self had?

Our pace slows while I try to process. How can a person be jealous of . . . herself? I glance up to the white goal post standing sentry over the end zone, and then suddenly, I get it. I know exactly how she feels, because I've been trying to compete with the other *me* too.

I take her hand and pull her through a gate onto the empty athletic field.

"C'mon."

"Where are we going?" She laughs nervously, but skips beside me across the turf.

We cross the fifty-yard line, and even now I'm drawn toward the home bench, but I keep going. There are weeds growing up through the lower section of the rickety wood and metal bleachers. Some of the seats are obstructed by an old announcer's box no one uses anymore except to climb into and get high. I keep going up into the stands. At the top we find a perfect view of the field and stretch of campus. It's dark and chilly, but up here it feels private.

Viv shivers. "Why did you want to come up here?"

I pull her down into my arms, leaning back against the rail. "To get you all to myself."

She twists in my lap until she's wrapped one leg around me, pressing her pelvis into mine, and it's all I can do to keep my response to just a groan.

The field looks completely different from this vantage. I'm used to being down *there*, not up here. I look out at the markings visible on the dark grass and try to picture the last game I played as it would've looked to someone in this spot. It's hard to detach myself from the action, to see a small ball flying into my arms—a small me so set on winning I don't see what's coming. Viv's frozen fingers find their way inside my shirt. A chill runs through me, but I let her warm them there.

"What are you thinking about?" she asks.

"I'm trying to remember what it was like to be him—before my leg."

"Ugh." She nuzzles into the open collar of my jacket. "*Practice, practice, practice* . . . then after the broken leg it was *physical therapy, weight lifting, practice* . . ."

I squeeze her. "I bet it was more like *Viv, practice, Viv, Viv, practice, Viv* . . ."

I lean in for a kiss but she pushes my face away playfully. "It wasn't."

"Well, if I were him, I'd—"

"You *are* him." She smiles crookedly.

"I wonder how our lives got to be so different. . . ."

She gazes down at me. "Because *you* did everything right."

I throw my head back and laugh. "I did everything wrong! I could've pushed myself to play . . . I wouldn't have been resented by the whole school—"

"What did you choose instead?" Viv asks, staring deep into my eyes.

"I . . . chose you." I realize it's true as soon as the words are out of my mouth. *Who needs them when we have each other?* I didn't think I'd need anything else, until the night she died.

She frowns, and there's such profound sadness in her eyes, I can barely stand it.

"Am I so bad?" she asks.

I wrap my arms around her and she leans in, hair spilling down around her face. Her lips are warm despite the chilly night.

"You're everything," I say.

She sits back and sniffs.

"Please let me stay here—forever?"

"Really, Viv"—I trace my finger down her perfect nose— "what's so complicated about your life?"

She hesitates and looks at her lap. "Everyone wants to judge me. I just want to get away from it all—with *you*."

I lift her chin and stare into her eyes. "I told you, we'll figure it out. You can't stay over here . . . but I'm not going anywhere."

She studies me back for a long second, but then her face falls and she slides out of my lap.

"Except to Nina's."

I sit motionless as the warmth where our bodies touched

slowly grows cold. I'd been prepared for something like this earlier, but now her tone of voice catches me completely off guard.

"Come on, Viv, I told you I wouldn't—"

"How am I supposed to know?"

"Are you still worried about the stalker thing? Because I don't think—"

She jerks her hand from my grasp. "I'm not!"

"But she tried to help me today—"

"She *what*?"

I realize what I've said far too late. Viv folds her arms tight in front of her.

"I didn't go to her—she came to see me." I take a deep breath, trying to calm myself. "Let's be reasonable."

She leaps up onto the wooden bench before I can blink. "You don't know her—you don't know what she did. She tried to take you from me—"

"Viv, get down." I get quickly to my feet. "You're going to fall."

The bleachers are old. There are no backs to the benches, just a low metal bar to keep *seated* people from falling off the back. Viv's eyes are wild, like an animal's. I've never seen her act this way before. She holds her arms out like she's on a balance beam, and teeters to one side. My eyes flit to the ground fifteen feet down, littered with broken glass.

Viv follows my gaze, leaning forward enough to edge my heart toward panic. Her expression is sad and ghostly. A breeze tosses her hair wildly across her face and I have this strange thought that if she just pushes it back, she'll be able to see that what she's doing, the way she's talking, is all wrong. But right then she does push it back—and that doesn't happen.

"I wonder if it hurt—when I died." She holds a fist to her chest and sways. "I don't think it could hurt like this."

My skin prickles with sweat, but the air doesn't feel cold anymore. I hold my hands up, heartbeat pounding out of control.

"*Okay!* I won't see her again—ever—please get down!"

Viv catches my eye and smiles. She moves to step down—but either loses her balance or changes her mind at the last second. I cry out. I don't know if she's going backward or forward; all I can see are her eyes, and she's falling, and—*we're in the front seat, she's reaching for the lighter, and the car is spinning and spinning across the pavement, and all I can do is close my eyes and*—I leap out and grab her Red Rams jacket, yanking her into my arms. We collapse into the aisle of the rickety bleachers in a heap, and I hold her so tightly, neither one of us can breathe.

"Just checking," she gasps.

I loosen my grip, but I don't let go.

TWENTY-SIX

I TUCK VIV SAFELY INTO BED AROUND MIDNIGHT, WITH A PROMISE on my lips to pick her up by nine tomorrow night. I lower the window behind me and walk slowly out to the road. Once my feet hit the blacktop, I let out a long breath I didn't even know I was holding. I feel empty, unsteady—completely drained. The evening keeps playing over in my mind, but each time I recall Viv—*my* Viv—standing at the top of those bleachers, I just get more confused. I need to go straight home to bed if I'm going to be worth anything tomorrow, but I take a right at the bottom of her street instead. I make it to Genesee Street in ten minutes, and it's another five until I'm standing in the last place I ought to be. In front of Nina's door.

I look over my shoulder before ringing the bell, which feels stupid and paranoid, and doesn't put me at ease. Viv was so upset tonight—there has to be something I'm missing. And Nina's the only person I know to ask. I tell myself it's okay to be here as long as it's for *us*. If I can figure out what's going on, I can fix it, and Viv will be happy.

Nina's actually in pajamas this evening, though her eyes tell me she hasn't been to sleep. Her loose gray pants have little penguins on them, and she's wearing this tight lacy blue camisole that doesn't seem to match. Not what I expected, and now I'm thrown. I was all ready to ask her about Viv, to try and get some insight on what happened tonight, but my thoughts scatter when I see her, and I chicken out.

"How's Owen?" I say. "Is he doing okay?"

"He's good . . . he's asleep." She hesitates, studies me for a long moment, and I'm sure she sees right through the *everything's fine* look I'm trying to keep on my face. "Do you want some tea?"

A part of me that's been winding tight all evening finally dares to relax. Tea. No drama or demands, just Nina and her open door.

In the kitchen, I swivel in one of the awkward yellow space-age chairs and Nina fills the kettle. She rests one hip against the cabinets while the water runs, looking away. I watch carefully. She sets out two mugs, selects tea, and refills the sugar, all without even a glance at me. She doesn't ask questions, doesn't seem at all alarmed that I'm there.

I have to sit on my shaking hands.

"I meant to come over sooner . . . to check on Owen."

She shrugs.

I flinch. There is no reason that should bother me, but the way she brushes me off, like it doesn't matter to her one way or the other, gets under my skin. I watch the blue flame flicker on the stove until the kettle whistles. Nina pours boiling water into the mugs, lets the tea steep, and adds two spoonfuls of sugar to mine without even pausing to ask. I smile, realizing she already knows exactly the way I like it.

"Thanks," I say, cupping the mug in one hand.

"My mom always used to say, there's no trouble so great that can't be diminished by a nice cup of tea." She smiles and shrugs. "You've probably heard that before."

"Not me," I say. Though when she said it, she almost scrunched her nose.

"She was English," she says. "One day I'm going to go there to the little village she came from. I want to live in the English countryside and read books, and invite people over for a nice cup of tea." She stops herself just as her voice gets dreamy. "Sorry."

"No, don't stop, it sounds nice."

She gives me a funny glance. "Sometimes I feel like I'm repeating myself."

I try to picture her living in a little cottage somewhere, but I'm not sure what else to include in an image of her being happy.

"So how would you spend your English countryside evenings?" I ask, remembering the posters in her closet. "Watching vintage horror films by yourself, or what?"

She looks up from her tea without lifting her head.

"Noticed your collection," I say lamely. "You've got good taste."

"You—*he* gave me those." She smiles at me tentatively. "We used to do that—a new horror flick every week. If we liked it, he'd track down a poster. I got a serious education in blood spatter and zombies."

I raise my eyebrows. "You need to know your zombies. But why not hang the posters?"

"I used to have them up all over." The smile retreats from her lips.

I think of her cell-like walls. "No offense, but your room is way scarier without them."

She snorts—but then it turns into a giggle. "That's why he bought them." Her cheeks go pink when she can't stop, and the laughter makes it all the way to her eyes. It's a good look for her.

Neither of us says anything for a while. She gets milk from the fridge and stirs it into her mug with a lingering smile. I settle into my chair. I was right to come. My troubles might not disappear with my tea, but being with Nina makes me feel better somehow.

My memory flashes back to why I came, and I sit forward, tense. The moment is gone.

"Why don't you and Viv like each other?" I ask.

Nina's eyes widen, but she hesitates before speaking.

"Why do you ask? Did she say something?"

"No, it's just . . . it seems that way," I say.

Her spoon clinks the edges of the mug loudly, around and around. I wish she'd stop. I can't think. Her back is straight, like she's ready to jump, but she looks down into the milky drink, not at me.

I gather the courage to say what I came here to say.

"Does Viv ever seem kind of . . . over the top to you?"

Nina's spoon clatters to the table, but she picks it back up. "I guess you could say that."

I wait for her to continue, but she just sits there, holding her spoon precariously over her mug. I can't get the image out of my mind of Viv teetering wild-eyed on the bleachers.

"She gets kind of reckless sometimes," I say.

"Um, wasn't she like that—"

"Before she died? Yeah, but it's not the same." I turn the idea over in my mind, trying to put my finger on what it could be. "She's always had an edge, but it was a fun one before. This is different."

"How?" Nina's features are a mask to me—so aggravating. Viv's face expresses everything she feels. At least I know what's going on with her even when I don't get why. I know Nina's never going to admit what she really thinks of Viv, but it would help if I could just figure out where she stands. I study her closely; she doesn't even twitch.

"I thought she was going to hurt herself tonight."

She looks up. "Hurt . . . herself?"

"I didn't know what to do, Nina. Viv—*my Viv*—would never have acted like that."

Saying it out loud makes me want to throw up.

"What did she do?" she asks stiffly.

I wave my hand and rest my elbow on the table. "It doesn't matter. She's okay. Look, I just need to know—is something going on between the two of you?"

She narrows her eyes. "Why would there be?"

"Don't ask me, I just got here!" I rake a hand through my hair. "Just, what did you do to piss her off? It's like she can read my mind if I'm even *thinking* about you."

Nina swallows hard. "She's never been a fan of our . . . friendship."

I clench my teeth and play the scenario on the bleachers over in my mind, Viv freaking about Nina, me lunging to catch her, the desperate look in her eyes. Every nerve in my body willing her not to fall. My eyes close. If I open them, I will be back there in the dark with her—on the bleachers, or in the car—the sky black and ready to swallow us both again. All I can hear is my own shallow breathing, drowning out the blood rushing through my ears.

"Cam?"

A warm hand closes over the top of mine. I jump and open my eyes. Nina's kitchen is bright and comfortable. Her eyes are questioning. I unclench my fists, and she gives the faintest smile. Something twinges deep in my chest.

She frowns. "Viv is kind of unbalanced . . ."

I rub my eyes and laugh. "Aren't we all?"

"That's not what I mean."

"I know, I can't really explain it either." I exhale, feeling stupid. But that twingey feeling won't leave. I place my palm back down next to hers, not quite touching it. "Sometimes I'm just not sure what she'll do next."

"I understand," she says.

"It's different with you."

Her cheeks flush, but she doesn't move away. She slides her hand back over to my hand, her brown eyes darting back and forth between mine. I get that *twinge* in my chest again, only this time I'm appalled because I recognize the feeling. My breath hitches—this is Nina—everything about it is wrong. I start to pull back, but her touch is so gentle, so calm, and then I remember . . . she's my *best friend*. I pause. Couldn't I have a special place for her, apart from Viv? I begin to wonder if this is how the other me felt.

Until she closes the distance between us and presses her mouth to mine.

My lips part automatically, my eyes fall closed, and for a moment it all makes sense. I lean into her—even as my brain catches up and my eyes pop open. Her other hand rests against my cheek and her eyes are squeezed shut in a way meant to prolong the moment. I shove my chair back hard to get away.

She stumbles, her face bright red. I stand abruptly, knocking the chair over.

"I—I'm sorry—" she says.

"Don't."

"Cam—I'm—"

"Stop!" I turn away. I can't look at her; I can't even think. We were talking about *Viv*, and then she—what did I do? I still taste her lips on mine. I wipe my mouth with my sleeve. "You were never going to tell me Viv was alive, were you? She tried to warn me—you *are* obsessed."

"What?" Her face goes white. "She said I'm—"

I get halfway to the front door, but she's on my heels.

"Cam—*Cam!*"

I whirl on her. "Look, I don't know what kind of fucked-up relationship you wanted with the other me, but you aren't a part of my life—Viv is."

She recoils, like I've hit her.

"Cam, please . . ." she whispers.

"Stop! Whatever sick fantasies you're still having about him, keep it to yourself!"

I throw the door open so hard, it crashes into the wall.

"But you're right about Viv—she's dangerous." Nina steps out on the porch and calls after me. "It's not too late, you could still get away. *He* would've believed me—"

Her voice fades as I storm into the night.

TWENTY-SEVEN

I HAVE THE STUPID DREAM AGAIN. EVERYTHING IS THE SAME—
the wreck, the fire—only this time Viv and I stand next to it,
together. She stares at the accident, clearly horrified, but then
she turns to me and her fear melts into a smile. I open my arms,
but suddenly I'm holding Nina. Viv sees her, stumbles and falls,
just as she did on the bleachers. I push Nina aside and dive to
catch her, but then I'm grabbing at empty air—and *I'm* falling
through blackness.

Alone.

I wake up sweating, heart pounding. I can barely move. I
feel like an offensive lineman is sitting on my chest. The dream
flashes through my mind again, and I have to walk myself
through my memories of last night to be sure I left Viv tucked
safely in her bed. I sit up and glance at the clock—3:26 a.m. I

wipe my face with the sheet, and then I remember Nina's kiss. I fall back onto the pillow. If only there was a way to make it unhappen, or even go back and pull away *faster*. I brushed my teeth and gargled as soon as I came home, but I rub a hand over my mouth again, as if there might still be some kind of evidence . . . something Viv might see.

I sit up and throw the covers off. My bed feels hot and stifling, so I open the window above me. The frozen air spills over me into the room, clearing my head. She'll never know it happened, how could she? Not unless Nina or I tell her, and Nina wouldn't. I clench my fist, thinking of her lips on mine—Viv never has to know about this, let alone forgive me for it.

I stare out into the darkness, confident for a moment before I slump against the sill. Maybe she should know. Viv and I never kept secrets from each other, so why would I start now? Nina kissed *me*—I didn't do anything wrong—I should have listened when Viv warned me about her. If I tell her what happened, she'll have to understand . . . she can't get upset with me for something I didn't do.

I shiver and close the window, sinking back into bed. The room is too cold now. I wrap myself in blankets against the chill and pull a pillow over my head, trying to decide what to do—lie or tell the truth?

I duck through the green light fast, banging my arm on its illusory edge. The impact is heightened by the electrical vibe, but I don't have time to think about it. I shouldn't have stretched out on my bed this afternoon, with as little sleep as I've had. The good news is, I woke up knowing I *have* to tell Viv what Nina did last night. I feel sick at the prospect of explaining exactly what happened, and I'm afraid of what she'll do, but I couldn't live with the lie. I want her to know she was right—I never should have doubted her. The bad news is, I've got five minutes to get to Viv's house, which is a ten-minute run from here.

I don't notice the car coming down the street until it pulls up next to me at the curb.

"Hey, hot stuff, need a ride?" Viv calls.

I do a double take, I can't help it. The last time I saw Viv's little blue two-door, it was wrapped around a pole. I survey it, as full of dings and dents as it ever was, but the front windows are rolled down, not shattered. I manage to find my voice.

"Sorry—I'm late. I . . . had to help my mom."

I bite my cheek. *What* is wrong with me? It took all day to decide to tell her the truth, and the first thing I do is lie right to her face?

"Well . . ." She smiles. "If it happens again, I might have to punish you."

I shiver, a little relieved. A small lie might be okay, in exchange for a big truth. She doesn't know I went to Nina's, or what happened there—yet. The car idles like it's grinding its teeth.

Viv coughs. "Are you going to get in, or should I wait till you stick your thumb out?"

I open the door, fighting off memories of the last time I performed this simple action. The very last time. She grabs some stuff off the seat, and I sit down, but I don't want to lean back. The car feels like a coffin.

"Cigarette?" she asks.

She has one balanced between her lips, and a red Bic in her hand. For a second I see my old silver Zippo instead, and my déjà vu climaxes—I snatch both away from her and throw them out the window.

"Hey! What the fuck was that for?"

"I . . ."

My throat burns like I just smoked a whole pack.

"You're not going to get all preachy, 'athletes-don't-smoke' at me again, are you? *You're* not an athlete anymore!"

I want to protest, but the sting in her tone keeps me from speaking. I've screwed up once already.

Her eyes move over me and she hesitates. I'm wearing the same clothes I had on yesterday, and I haven't shaved.

"You look like shit, Cam. What's wrong with you tonight?"

"Can we go somewhere . . . to talk?" I manage to ask.

Her fingers tighten on the wheel. "About what? We can talk here."

I glance out the window, at the corner where *I* died.

"Let's go somewhere with less traffic. I want us to be alone."

She quirks an eyebrow and puts the car in gear. "Well, when you put it like that, I know *just* the place."

We twist through the streets behind school for a while, the car squealing around corners, climbing uphill. I slide the seat belt into place across my lap and try not to make it obvious I'm gripping the door handle in one sweaty palm. I play with the radio with my free hand. There's only one hill in *or* around Fayetteville. I know exactly where we're going.

"The water tower?"

"For old times' sake," she says, and presses her lips together.

There are fewer houses the higher we get, and more sparsely leaved trees. It's no mountain or anything, but I guess no one wants to live that close to a giant ugly tank covered in graffiti. Especially when it's the hottest make-out spot for miles.

We used to come every time we won a game, and there were a lot of wins sophomore year. There's only one other car when we get to the dirt lot at the top, but it's dark and looks either empty or abandoned. Viv rolls far enough toward the edge of the lot that we can see the lights of Fayetteville below. I've never spent much time actually admiring the view from this place. It's beautiful.

"I forgot what it was like to come up here with you," I say.

"Yeah, me too." Viv yanks on the parking brake. She reaches for her cigarettes, thinks better of it, and turns off the ignition.

I hold the pack out to her. "You can smoke—I shouldn't have done that before."

"I don't want one now." She drums her fingers on the wheel.

I know she's waiting for me to just say whatever I want to talk about, but I can't make myself do it. I stare out at the stars suspended over the town.

"Do you ever wonder if *they're* together?" I ask.

She stops drumming and looks at me. "Who?"

"Our other . . . selves? Like, if they're both dead, and we're alive, do you think they get to be together too?"

She tilts her head and follows my gaze into the sky. "No."

"Really? You think they're alone—or just gone?"

"No, I don't wonder about it."

"Oh."

She takes my hand. "Cam, you *are* him, only better. . . . Aren't I enough like her?"

I think for a moment, studying her face. Her smile vanishes.

"You're like her in so many ways. . . ."

"But?"

I hesitate, trying to find the right words.

"But nothing—you're my Viv." I squeeze her hand to make her feel better. Or do I need reassuring? "Which is why I wanted to tell you . . . you were right about Nina."

She stares at me. I look down at my lap.

"I went to see her last night."

She gasps. "But you—"

"I'm sorry—I had to find out for myself!"

She jerks her hand out of mine and crosses her arms over her chest. I panic and try to reach for her, but she pulls back as far as she can in the seat and balls up fistfuls of her jacket. I watch in horror as her face starts to crumple.

"It was awful—you were right!" I say hastily. "She's crazy, totally obsessed. One minute we were talking, the next . . . she's trying to kiss me."

Viv's eyes turn to daggers.

"You *kissed* her?"

"No! She kissed me!"

"How could you?"

"I didn't!" The windows are fogged from the heat of our breath, making me feel even more boxed in. "I was trying to help *us*!"

I hear her hand hit my cheek an instant before I feel it burn into my skin. She reaches for the door, but I grab her shoulders.

"Viv, listen to me!"

I don't know what to say to make this right. I pull her to me, pressing my mouth against hers, but her lips don't respond. I tangle my fingers through her hair, locking her into my kiss until I can barely breathe.

When I lean back, she looks at me like I'm dead.

"You've got to understand." My voice cracks in desperation.

"No, *you've* got to," she says. There's no spark left in her eyes. "*He* left *me* for *her*—I tried to tell you last night."

The wind is knocked out of my lungs. If my face weren't still stinging I might think she punched me in the gut instead.

"What?"

She closes her eyes, pained.

"That's ridiculous," I say, "I would never—"

"*He* did."

I brace my elbows on my knees, holding my head in my hands. I try to imagine a scenario where I might have left Viv—for *anyone*—but I come up blank. Blood rushes into my face. This is impossible. He and I might have lived differently, but we were still the same person. It's like he betrayed both of us.

"It was Nina," Viv says in answer to my thoughts. "She did

something to him, turned him against me." She looks up, eyes gleaming. "And then he died. I thought everything was over; I wanted to die too . . . but then you came back to me."

I reach for her, and this time she doesn't pull away. "I'm *not* him."

We kiss until we're out of breath. I run my lips down her neck, her pulse drumming steadily beneath her skin. Her fingers are cool and magnetic, twined with mine. She slides my jacket off, and I'm pulling her shirt over her head while she wrestles with my belt. Something inside me seems to vibrate at her touch. I shed my sweater and try to move in closer to her skin, but I bang my bad knee on the steering wheel. I pull away and bite my cheek until the pins and needles stop resonating through me. By the time the pain dissipates, Viv's reclined in her seat. She studies me curiously, eyelids heavy, a strand of hair twirled around her finger.

"Cam," she says with a seductive smile. "I've been wondering. Did you and I ever . . . ?"

My face gets so hot, I've never been more thankful for the dark of night. I have to look away from her bare, smooth silhouette. Things are different enough for each of us, why has this thought never crossed my mind?

"No—" My voice breaks and I clear my throat. "That's where we were going. The night of the crash."

"Oh . . ."

I wait for what feels like an interminable second. "Did you?"

"Never had the chance." Her voice is low with regret.

I let out a long sigh, relieved.

She shivers and rubs her arms.

"You're freezing, aren't you?"

I dig around until I find the sweater I'd been wearing, and drape it over her naked midriff. She pulls it to her nose and inhales, wrapping herself in my sleeves. But then she props herself up on one elbow and juts out her lower lip.

"I'm sick of sneaking around this way—cramped in my car, shivering on the playground. It's getting old fast."

I shrug, reaching to tickle her toes. "We can't risk being seen . . . again."

She smiles, obviously scheming. "What if we had a whole house to ourselves—a great big bed, a warm fireplace, and I could guarantee no one would ever find us?"

I recline my seat and move as close to her as the center console will allow.

"I'd say tell me where and when."

She grins. "My parents will be gone all night Friday—totally last-minute, some business colleague died. I was going to tell you first thing." She sits up, and my sweater falls into her lap. Her skin is illuminated by the soft glow of a light mounted high on the water tower. I'm used to her hair cascading down around her shoulders, but with her curls in disarray high up around her chin, I get an uninterrupted view of her nearly naked torso. The only thing between me and the soft rise of her breasts is a very purple, very revealing, very sexy lace bra.

She leans over. "Come spend the night with me."

I shift uncomfortably, no longer bothered by the cold. "What's wrong with right now?"

She runs her hand down my bare chest, alerting every nerve beneath my skin.

"I want our first time to be special . . . not some fling in my backseat."

I exhale and bite my lip, trying not to focus on how good she looks . . . what it does to me. It seems like an eternity since the night when it *should* have happened. Our eyes connect, and I envision all the times it nearly did. She must see it on my face, because even in the dim light, I can tell she's blushing. The air heats between us and I catch her hand in mine—maybe this is just what we need. This one thing to seal us together and erase all the doubt.

TWENTY-EIGHT

HALF OF THURSDAY BLURS BY IN A WHIRL OF BLANK FACES,
bells ringing, and lockers slamming. I barely pass a trig test and
survive a second round of dodge ball in the morning. If I can get
an essay written before fifth period history, I'll be caught up on
assignments for the week, but my mind keeps jumping ahead to
Friday night.

When I finally make it to lunch, I stake out the usual doorway and pull out a notebook and pen. I'm supposed to answer
the question, *In* Ethan Frome, *what is the significant realization
that Ethan makes?* I've filled about half a page when a flat silver
object skitters across the floor and knocks into my shoe. I pick up
the cell phone and glance around for its owner, but the scowling
person coming toward me with his hand out is Logan.

I hold the phone up. "Lose something, West?"

"Hand it over, Pike."

He's angry—I bet I can make him angrier. I toss the cell phone into the air.

Logan scrambles, surprised. He reaches out, actually has it, but then it slips between his fingers. I catch it again before it hits the floor.

I get to my feet. "Fumble."

Logan's face goes as red as our school's mascot. I hold the cell out to him. Several groups of people are watching now to see if I get my ass kicked. I wonder if *this* Logan would freak out if he ran into Viv; if he'd dare lay claim to her "ghost." The thought relaxes me and I'm not sure I feel like sinking my fist into his face anymore.

"Shame you have to lose this season without me," I say, slapping him on the shoulder.

He balls up his fists, nostrils flaring . . . but then Tash appears beside him and takes one of his hands. He looks at her, back at me, and something in his posture changes. He sticks the phone in his pocket and, still holding Tash's hand, pushes away through the cluster of gathered people.

Mike shoves through the dispersing crowd. "What the hell was that?"

"Never mind," I say, settling stiffly on the floor, sore from the twenty push-ups I did this morning. I might not be a player anymore, but I can still look good on Viv's arm. Mike scowls at me and starts walking away. I pick my notebook up, then toss it back down and jog after him.

"Mike!"

He turns. He's chomping on an energy bar.

"If my mom calls your place Friday night . . . tell her I'm there."

He stops chewing. "You want *me* to cover for you?"

"Yeah."

"Why should I?"

It sinks in now that he's pissed. And why wouldn't he be? All I've done lately is act like a dick to him.

"Look, I'm sorry," I mumble. "It's important. I wouldn't ask if it wasn't."

His expression changes. "Who's the girl?"

"Girl? There's no—" I collect myself. "Yes or no?"

"Cam, I think you owe me. I'm not doing this for free."

I glare at him, but he doesn't blink. I wrinkle up my forehead in frustration. There's no time for this. After Friday, everything will be okay again—better than okay. But my night with Viv has to be perfect. Nothing can get in the way. I force myself to unclench my jaw. It's just a detail, but so much is at stake. If one thing goes wrong . . . it could ruin more than our night. I consider pleading, but he just stands there and waits.

"You're right," I say, surprising myself. "I do owe you."

He studies me like he's trying to decide if I'm bullshitting him, but I guess he's satisfied with the look on my face.

"Fine, whatever. I've got your back."

TWENTY-NINE

MOM'S CAR IS IN THE DRIVEWAY WHEN I GET HOME. THIS NEVER used to be a good sign after school, but she's been around a lot more since she started trying to be maternal. She's even making an effort to keep the place clean. Her shower is running when I walk in the front door, so I head for the kitchen to hunt down some food.

I've got my hand on the fridge when the new phone blares its digitized ring from the opposite wall. I pick up the receiver, cradling it against my shoulder as I open the door to browse.

"Hello?"

"Cam?"

I freeze with a can of V8 in my hand.

"Don't hang up—can we talk?"

Dad's voice sounds unsteady. I don't breathe.

"Look, I've been trying to get ahold of you—"

"How's that going for you?"

The line goes quiet. Why did I speak? My thumb hovers over the end button.

"I bought the boat back, Cammer."

He what?

I clamp my hand over my mouth before I can say anything.

"Mom says things have been tough lately. I thought maybe . . ." He sighs. "I thought you might like to go out on the lake?"

I stand there like a moron, holding on to the phone, but I swallow so he knows I'm there.

"You don't have to decide now. The weather will hold."

I open my mouth and pause, thinking of me and Dad on our boat, rocking lazily on the water. I can almost smell the trout. I want to cry *Yes!* But I also want a reason not to.

"Would Cheryl come too?"

"Nope," he says. "Just you and me."

I sink into a kitchen chair. It used to be so much easier to hate him. But ever since the accident . . . it's like he's called almost every day.

"You got the *Reel Fun* back?"

He coughs. "Lost a little money in the deal, but I'm hoping it'll be worth it."

I scan the open newspaper without reading it.

"I miss hanging out with you, buddy. . . ."

"Yeah." My chest gets heavy at his words. "Well—I gotta go."

"Just think about it," Dad says. "Take all the time you want."

I click the phone off without moving. I can't believe I let him win. I open my eyes, and my mom is standing in the doorway, her head wrapped in a towel.

"How'd it go?" she asks.

"You knew he was going to call?"

"I thought it would be a good idea for you two to talk."

"Why?" I ask, incredulous. "You should hate him more than I do."

She tugs at the sleeve of her bathrobe. "He's not quite the asshole he used to be."

"Mom! He left you for that—"

"You don't have to remind me!"

I shake my head, trying to control my temper. "So, are you trying to pass me off on him, or what?"

"Excuse me?"

I gesture to the stack of dishes that have reappeared in the sink. "Life is hard enough, but if you can get rid of me—"

"No one's suggesting you move in with him."

"Then why talk to him at all?"

The towel falls sideways on her head. "He's your dad, Cam."

"Does he want an award?"

She sighs and pulls a pack of cigarettes out of her pocket. "I got to draw up my own divorce papers—I have an excuse never to see him again." She tilts her head. "But you share DNA with him. He's the only dad you've got."

I grunt and stick the phone back in its cradle.

She fumbles for a light. I hand her a matchbook from a drawer.

I open the fridge door again, but I'm not hungry anymore. I find myself thinking about Owen, and I wonder if it's worse to have a shitty dad or no father at all. I close the fridge door. Mom hung a picture of Viv there—the one I took at sunset. Somehow looking at it still makes me sad. As if she's really gone . . . and I don't have her back.

"What are you even doing home?" I ask. "It's only four o'clock."

"I had a court date tomorrow, but it got pushed to next week," she says. "I thought I'd kick back and work in my pajamas till then . . . spend the weekend with my kid."

I straighten. "Um, I kind of have plans—with Mike."

"Oh." She blinks at me. "But you haven't . . . in months."

"Part of my improvement package? I'll be at his house Friday night." I resist the urge to look away when I say this. You should never break eye contact with a lawyer when you're lying.

"Mike Liu? I haven't seen him in forever. Why don't you guys come over here? It'll be fun, like old times!"

I shake my head. "No—we're doing guy stuff. You wouldn't want us here." This is lame, I need specifics. . . . "Video games! The new *Zombies versus Aliens*—I don't have the game console. He's got it all at his house, so . . . we have to go there."

She raises one eyebrow. My stomach sinks.

"Well, you won't mind if I call and talk to his mother—what's her name again?"

I can't speak as she plucks the phone off the wall. My palms are moist. Not because I'm worried about Mrs. Liu blowing my cover, that's a given now. My mind is leaping to the next unknown—how Viv will react when she finds out I can't come. What she'll do.

Mom fusses with the number, and I don't help her. She gets it from directory assistance—there's only one Liu family in town—and it starts ringing. I have time to hope it'll go to voice mail, but then her blank expression perks up and she smiles.

"Mrs. Liu? Oh, this isn't—oh, Nicole! You sound so grown up. For a second you sounded *just* like your mom . . . is she there?"

I get my bullshit from my mother.

"Oh, I see. No, that's okay, this is Loretta Pike—Camden's mom? Just tell her to call me when she gets a chance—"

Pause. A glance at me.

"I'll let him know, sweetie." She laughs. "Okay, thanks, bye."

My heart, barely pumping a second ago, now dares to shift back into hopeful mode.

"Mike's little sister says she thinks you're cute." She winks.

"Uh, great." I glance at the phone, calculating how soon football practice ends so I can give Mike a heads-up. I push my chair back and stand. "Well, I have a ton of homework. Guess you'll have to check up on me some other time."

She cocks her head and holds out her arms. "Come here, you. I'm proud of how hard you're trying. Go see your friends and get out a little, have fun."

I hesitate, letting the guilt creep in. Things were easier when she didn't try so hard to care. I bury her in my arms, breathing in the scent of her shampoo mixed with cigarettes and her mom-perfume. I've never gotten used to bending down for her hugs, and even now I worry I might accidentally crush her. When I let go, she pinches my cheek like she hasn't done since I was six.

"Ow!" I rub my face.

"Your turn to do the dishes."

THIRTY

"JUST LET ME IN—THEY WON'T HEAR US," I PLEAD.

Viv leans out the window, silencing me with her full, luscious mouth. She lingers playfully on my lower lip before placing a hand on my forehead and gently shoving me back.

"I told you . . . they've got their lawyer over for dinner tonight. He'll be here late." She rolls her eyes, but glances over her shoulder at the door. "I have to go be the obedient daughter."

I cock one eyebrow. "Since when are you obedient?"

She laughs, but covers her mouth and hushes me.

"We have the place to ourselves all night tomorrow. Mr. Winters is checking in on me Saturday morning, but you can hide. They won't be back till afternoon."

"Their *lawyer* is checking in on you? Since when did they get so concerned?"

"Since . . . you died." She looks at the ground. "Anyway, it's no big deal. He's practically my uncle."

I sigh, and lower myself from tiptoe.

She leans down to kiss me again, and the view from where I stand is a promise in pink satin. I groan into her neck.

"I'm gonna go take a cold shower."

She pulls the window closed with a sensuous smile. "It'll be worth the wait . . . I promise."

I walk down the middle of a dark, empty street, trying to shake off my arousal. My body aches for Viv, but in the best possible way, buzzing with anticipation. Friday night never felt so far away. Everything's going to be perfect now; I know it will.

I make it back to the utility pole, and let my fingers tingle and glow, illuminating the school—*my* school—through a green filter in front of Viv's. I breathe a silent thank-you, again, for this weird window's existence and all its strange parallels. Then I push my way toward home.

I'm about halfway through the light when I get stuck. The electricity humming through my skin is so disorienting, I feel around to find the edges of the space I'm in, and they're a lot closer than I remember—claustrophobic. I turn sideways, find a place where I can poke my hand through, then push and duck until I find my way out. I stumble into the dark, kneel on the sidewalk, and cough. Lingering in there can't be good for anyone's health.

"Have trouble fitting through this time?"

I stand up quickly, forcing my eyes to adjust from green light back to night. Nina sits on a rock two feet away, bundled up in a hooded jacket like she's been waiting there awhile.

"Stay away from me," I say, and start walking home.

"It's getting smaller, Cam. I think it's going to close."

I stop in my tracks, panic shooting through me . . . until I realize what she's doing.

"This isn't going to work—you just sound desperate."

She comes toward me, unsmiling. "Maybe I am."

I step back.

Nina laughs, but there's no humor in it.

"At first I just assumed I forgot what it was like to squeeze through, but I tried it again tonight, and that thing's definitely getting smaller."

"You're lying," I say quickly. But something in her voice unsettles me.

She comes close enough that she has to look up at me, and her hood falls back. I expected her face to be blotchy from crying or just being crazy, but her skin is pale and clear, her hair smooth and pretty.

"Don't believe me?" she asks. "You've been coming through a lot more than me . . . but you might have been too preoccupied to notice."

I glance doubtfully at the pole. I am in a hurry whenever I'm here. It feels like years since the first time I went through to find Nina. But I remember that experience clearly—I was terrified, but it was easy, like walking through a door. I run my hand through my hair, recalling the last several times I've gone back and forth. Times I've had to twist, bend, or almost got stuck. I cover my mouth.

"If that thing closes—" She gestures toward the utility pole. "You *can't* be on the same side with her."

My mood darkens. She's only telling me this to keep us apart—to try and take me away from Viv all over again. I lean forward. "You're. A. Lunatic."

She closes her eyes and clenches her teeth. "I saw you come through just now—you know I'm right about this!"

I start to walk again, fast, but Nina's voice cuts into my back.

"It was a blue car," she says.

I stop.

"The hit-and-run that killed you. They were driving a blue car . . . just like Viv's."

It takes several moments for her words to make any kind of sense in my brain. Finally, an image of Viv behind the wheel flashes through my head so clear, every muscle in my body goes rigid, as if bracing for impact. I want to blink, close my eyes, but I can't. My own frozen breath swirls white and ghostly through the air in front of me, then disappears. It's hard to breathe back in.

"How would you know?" I ask.

"Because—I saw it happen. I was on my way to meet you here." A single tear runs down the smooth skin of her cheek. "And . . . I didn't make it in time."

A tingle runs down my spine, like the fingers of a ghost. I stare at her, waiting for her to flinch. She doesn't. I glance away, at the corner, and a weight settles in the middle of my chest. Is she desperate enough to make something like this up?

"You're lying."

"I never saw her face, only the car—but she found out about us, Cam, she *knew*—"

"Shut up!"

She presses her lips together and just looks at me. I turn away so I can't see her face, and she can't see mine.

"There's a hearing on Monday . . . I have to tell them what I saw."

I whirl to face her. "A *court* hearing? For what?"

She takes a deep breath. "To determine whether or not your death was accidental."

My hands are shaking. I shove them in my pockets, but it doesn't help.

"Viv would have told me about anything that serious."

Nina tilts her head. "Would she?"

I hesitate, staring down the street where the pavement disappears into blackness. Even if Viv did hit me, it *had* to have been an accident.

"Look, I didn't want to tell you any of this, but if you stay— I'm afraid it'll happen again."

I ball up my fists. It's all I can do to speak without screaming.

"It's not going to happen, Nina, because I'm *never* leaving Viv for you! Get it through your head, we will Never. Be. Together."

Her voice takes on an edge. "I lost you once already. I know I'm going to lose you again. But if I know you're safe here, and she's stuck over there with me—"

"Don't you *dare* try to keep her from me."

She stomps her foot. "Damn it, Cam, have you been listening to a word I've said?"

"Accusing Viv of murder? That's what you're sinking to?"

She comes forward and jabs her finger at my chest. "*You* were the one telling me how she seems over the top sometimes, how you aren't sure what she'll do next."

"Yeah, right before you threw yourself at me."

She throws her head back. "Sometimes I forget what an ass you are and mistake you for him."

I kick the bushes to my right. My knee throbs in protest, as if to mock me further. I point to the corner. "If that thing closes, you can bet I'll be on this side—with Viv—far away from you."

I turn my back on her and head down the sidewalk.

"No!" Her footsteps hurry after me. "Look, I don't know what your Viv was like. Maybe she didn't get possessive and try to isolate you; maybe without me around she didn't try to keep you all to herself—"

"Stop it!"

"Just don't get them confused!"

"Don't you dare talk about her." My voice seems small and lost out in the open. I glance automatically to where the shrine used to be.

"I'm sorry," she says, following my gaze. She wraps her arms around herself and sighs, staring at the pavement. "I couldn't save *his* life, but I thought I might be able to save yours. I've never had a second chance—at anything."

I feel her eyes on me, but I refuse to look at her.

"I did love him," she murmurs. "No matter what else you think."

She turns away and starts walking back to the corner. When she gets to the pole, I watch her reach one hand out steadily until it goes transparent. She slips her arm in, angles sideways, and squeezes through a very narrow shaft of green light.

She doesn't even look back before she disappears.

This corner is dark and empty. That's all it used to be, and I realize, all it will be again soon. I walk up to where Nina vanished, and catch the peach scent of her hair. I reach into the darkness, trailing green fingertips through the air. I trace the edges of what once felt like a doorway to forever but now feels like a tiny window about to close.

Nina's words echo through my mind.

A blue car.

THIRTY-ONE

TONIGHT THE DREAM IS DIFFERENT. I'M ON THE CORNER ALONE.
Once again there's no sound, and I can't move. Something catches
my eye—a figure in the distance. Nina? She's running and waving, but she can't seem to get any closer. I try to call out to her, but
I have no voice. I turn my head away, glimpse a blur of blue, and
am blinded by white light.

I wake shivering in my bed, staring at a black sky. The window
above me is wide open. Startled, I close it, and wipe my forehead
with my T-shirt. I'm dripping with sweat. I strip to my boxers
and burrow back under my blankets, but it's impossible to relax
or sleep.

Not after that dream.

I never asked Viv *or* Nina about the hit-and-run . . . it seemed
straightforward. The person got scared and ran—I assumed they

were never caught. But now I'm afraid to wonder. Because Viv's mentioned regretting bad things that she's done. And sometimes it seems like she's running from her world. And sometimes her jealousy seems a lot like fear.

But who could blame her for feeling that way? It was a terrible *accident*.

How could Nina suggest it was anything else?

I walk into the shadows at the corner and let them swallow me, making sure the coast is clear in every direction. I'm not taking any chances tonight. There was a football game this evening, but it was away, thank God.

An arctic blast has moved down from the north, freezing everything. It feels like ice crystals are forming in my lungs. My heart races when I reach into the empty, black space next to the utility pole. I exhale as my hand slides into its familiar transparent green glove.

Will this be the last time? Will I get home again—with Viv? I try not to think about it.

I trace the outline of the space with my right hand, taking in the dimensions as best I can. It looks smaller than yesterday, but I can't really tell. I can't believe I needed Nina to make me notice it at all.

I glance over my shoulder one more time, but she's not here. And if she knows what's good for her, she won't be when Viv and I come back, either. Because after I sort this stuff about the accident out, Viv and I will leave here, together. I slip one foot through the sliver of pale green light, duck down holding my breath, and squeeze with some difficulty to the other side. Maybe for once it's good that I don't weigh what I did two years ago. I let the energy dissipate—even that doesn't seem to last as long—and I glance around.

My teeth chatter. It seems even colder here, on Viv's corner. It's eerie, dark, and alone, the way mine—*ours*—felt at home on the other side. Ours. Soon our worlds won't be *his* and *hers* anymore. We'll be together in one place from now on.

Where am I going to *hide* her?

A car revs its engine a street or two away, shaking me out of my thoughts. I tense and wait, but it doesn't come any closer. A shudder runs through me. *A blue car.* Those three words have haunted me since Nina claimed she saw it happen. I wonder what I was really doing on this corner alone, in the middle of the night. Viv agrees that I—*he*—left her for Nina, and Nina says we were supposed to meet here on the corner. . . .

There is no way Viv was behind the wheel of that car. It was probably a drunk driver. Drunk drivers hit people randomly all the time.

A wind sweeps through my jacket, and I shiver against it.

The hit-and-run that killed you. They were driving a blue car. . . .

I have to talk to Viv. Now.

By the time I glimpse the glowing yellow light in Viv's window, I can barely close my fingers to rap on the glass. I cough, trying to free my lungs from this choke hold of winter. The shade goes up, the window opens, and Viv peeks outside.

"Wow, it got cold!" She crosses her arms in front of her.

I forget everything as soon as I get a look at her. Despite the weather where I'm standing, she's dressed in red boy shorts and a tiny matching camisole that leaves little to my imagination. I blow on my hands. Nothing like getting my blood pumping again.

"Hi . . ." I say unabashedly to her cleavage.

She laughs. "Go around front—I'll meet you at the door."

She moves from the window, and without the vision of her to occupy me, my brain is jolted back to the shrinking green light. I stumble quickly around the side of the house. She holds the door wide open and hurries me inside. She takes my icy hand in hers and guides me to the living room in front of a roaring fire.

I gaze at her as she gently rubs my fingers and blows on them.

How could Nina ever think Viv is capable of murder?

"There, is that better?" she asks, slipping off my jacket. "Hey, where's all your stuff?"

I hesitate, making a production of warming myself by the fire.

"No toothbrush, no pj's?" She raises an eyebrow. "Will you be sleeping in the buff?"

"I didn't think we'd need a whole lot of . . . accessories," I say. If I do this carefully, maybe she won't freak out. I move to the couch and pull her into my lap. She smells amazing. Her legs stretch out, endless and smooth in front of me.

I tear my eyes away and blink several times. God, I need to focus.

"Wasn't your mom and dad's lawyer coming by or something?"

"It's under control." She runs her fingers under the edge of my shirt, setting my skin on fire. I lose concentration. "Oh, I snagged you a six-pack from my dad's supply in the garage. . . ."

She gets up and hurries out of the living room before I can stop her. I sit up and rub a hand over my face. I should've gotten straight to the point when I walked in. She returns a moment later and pops open two cans.

"Maybe we should go . . . to my room?"

I glance past her down the hall that leads to her bedroom and imagine her soft pink bedspread and pictures all over the walls—except I have to remind myself they won't be the images in my memory. The ones on her wall in this world are full of strange faces, people I'm not used to, and things I never did. That shot of the Red King and Queen is directly over her bed.

"It's nice here," I say hastily. "Maybe in a little while?"

"Oh . . . okay." She sits down next to me and hands me a beer. "To second chances."

"Second chances," I echo. The beer is bitter and weak. I swallow fast. "Viv, I . . ."

"Shh . . ."

Her fingers trace their way up my thigh, running along the waistband of my jeans while she lays kisses all the way up my neck to my mouth. I close my eyes, distracted, tasting the cherry ChapStick on her lips. I should stop her—I will—in a second. How many months have I longed for this? I lean back, running my hand up over her shoulder blades to her hair, and let myself dissolve into her skin. Her scent surrounds me, warm, familiar, and comforting. I don't think I realized what it was like to miss her until this moment.

She shifts, and the side of the couch digs into my back. I ignore it. She tilts her head, smiles, and reaches for my belt.

I take a deep breath, trying to shut off my brain. This is actually going to happen. We can talk—after.

Viv straddles my lap, putting all her weight on my right knee. *"Ow!"*

I jerk my leg up instinctively, and almost clip her chin. She scrambles back to the other end of the couch, eyes wide.

"What's wrong with you?" she asks.

I trace the edge of her shorts regretfully with my eyes, and sigh.

"The light . . . the window through . . . whatever you want to call it, it's getting smaller."

She frowns. "So?"

"At the corner—Viv, we can't go back and forth anymore."

She sits forward. My disjointed explanation must be sinking in. "What are you talking about? Of course we can."

I shake my head. "I barely got through tonight."

Her eyes widen. "But—*why?*"

"I don't know!"

She jumps up from the couch, knocking a pillow to the floor. "Then we have to go!"

A knot forms in my stomach. She's right; we should get up now and *go* . . .

"We will, but Viv—"

"Why didn't you tell me sooner?" She dashes toward the hall, stops, then lurches back toward me, frantic. "It can't close before we leave! I can't stay here! We have to go!"

"I didn't know—" It's like a cloud has settled inside my head. "Viv, we can't go yet."

She brushes a strand of hair from the corner of her mouth and looks at me like my head is on backward. She glances at the door, but stays where she's standing, breathing hard.

"Why?"

I wet my lips and look back up at her. The edge of her camisole has ridden up to reveal bare skin just above the rise of her shorts.

I can't take it. My *body* chickens out.

"You'll never be able to come back, as far as I know," I say quickly. "Your parents and all your friends might think—"

She cuts me off. "Are you joking?"

"No."

Viv glares at the ceiling and rakes a hand through her carefully styled hair. But then she closes her eyes and makes an obvious effort to breathe more slowly. She straightens her top and marches back over, positioning herself next to me on the couch.

"Cam, how many times can I tell you?" She takes my hand. "I don't care."

The knot in my gut twists at her touch. Her voice may be calm, but her eyes are resolved.

"I know, I just thought—"

"Don't you want me?" Her voice is small.

My palms go clammy. "Of course I do!"

"Then . . . what are you saying?" she asks. She traces lines across my palm, but her grasp is tight. She lifts her gaze to meet mine and her eyes are steely. "You're trying to go back without me?"

"Never." I squeeze her hand, trying to stay calm, but my words come out panicked. "I just don't want you to have any regrets."

"Regrets." She tightens her grip on me until it starts to become uncomfortable. "Do *you* have any regrets?"

A blue car.

The thought enters my mind at the worst possible moment. I force my gaze down, afraid Viv will be able to tell. I turn her hand over in mine. Her fingers are long and slender; her nails are filed and polished. These hands couldn't kill . . .

But then I picture her knuckles white, gripping a steering wheel.

"Viv . . ." I speak carefully. "I know what happened that night."

The words are out, hanging between us. Hers now, to confirm or deny.

"I don't know what you're talking about." She jerks away from me, gets up, and walks to the other end of the room. She snatches a cigarette from her father's desk, but whirls around and strides back with it unlit in her hand. "Did *Nina* say something? She's a liar, she's obsessed—"

"I—I just want to understand," I stammer. "Viv, please . . ."

She looks at me long and hard, then she takes a matchbook off an end table, strikes twice, and lights up. She takes a drag and tosses her curls, putting one hand on her hip. She inspects something on her arm that only she can see, and brushes it away.

Then slowly, shakily, she sinks back onto the couch next to me and closes her eyes.

"*He* didn't want to understand." She opens her eyes and lets her fingers trace down my throat to my chest. "I've missed touching you so much."

My heart hammers like it might race right out of my body, but my skin stays cold. I want to scream for her to say something else. This can't be what she means . . . what it sounds like.

"So," I say, struggling to keep my voice calm. "You did it—"

"He didn't know what he wanted." Her voice breaks. "She tried to take you away from me."

The knot inside me pulls so tight, I feel like I'm being cut in two. I'm not sure if she's talking about *him* or *me* anymore, but I don't think it matters. I can't move.

She sets the cigarette in an ashtray and pulls closer, wrapping her arms around my waist. My muscles tense. She runs her fingers up my arm, my neck, and starts playing with my hair like she's bewildered that I'm really there. I stare down at this face I know so well. These deep brown eyes, full lips, and arching brows. I know every flicker of fear, doubt, or affection that's ever crossed these features. But when I look into her eyes now—I see a stranger.

I feel sick; it hurts to breathe. The elation of when I first saw her again—all the renewed hope for the future—seems to crack and splinter. I clench my hands, but pain spreads up my arms, into my body, working its way through each muscle and bone.

"Cam?"

"*She* would never have done that to me. . . ." I whisper.

"If she loved you as much as I do, she would have." Her voice is calm. "So no one else could have you."

I can't move. I can't speak.

She sits up fast. "But that doesn't matter! Not now! We'll go through to your side and start over—Tahiti, Cam! It'll be like nothing ever happened!" Her voice cracks. "You already quit football like I said you should, there won't be anyone there to interfere. It'll just be the two of us. . . ."

I close my eyes. "Because who needs them when we have each other?"

"Exactly!"

I blink hard. Those places to go, things we dreamed, were gone before we ever shared them. I just never knew it. I rise from the couch and walk to the front door.

"Wait . . . where are you going?" Viv comes running after me. "Cam!"

I open the door and a blast of cold air blows over us, into the house—or at least it must be cold, by the way she shrieks and tries to push the door closed. All I feel is numb.

"Cam, it's freezing!" She wraps her arms around herself, trying to cover her sensuous, dangerous curves. "Close the door and help me pack!"

I shake my head because she doesn't *get it*. I push the door away from her with an unsteady hand, and that's when I realize I'm not numb at all—I'm completely terrified. I step outside, and she flies out the door after me, hanging off my arm.

"Where are you going? Cam, come inside! Please—" she wails. "Cam, please, it was an accident—*I tried to stop*—"

Her feet are bare. She digs her heels in, but then she drags along the ground crying, and I just wish she'd let go—because every time I dreamed of having her on my arm, it never looked like this. A few lights come on across the street. It starts to snow as I hit the sidewalk.

"I'm so sorry," she sobs.

Tears burn the corners of my eyes. I jerk her off my arm and hear her fall into a heap on the ground. I can't look at her—I can't see.

I run.

THIRTY-TWO

I THINK I'M HEADED TOWARD THE SCHOOL. THE STREETS AND HOUSES look right, but whenever I focus too hard everything in front of me starts to blur. I just keep going. Faint white flakes keep floating past my face. I left my jacket at Viv's, but there's no way I'll go back for it now. I pull my sleeves over my fingers and listen to my shoes hit the pavement in a sad, slow rhythm.

Nina was right.

This thought breaks through the hum of my movement, clear and shrill. But there's nothing I can do about it now. I have to get home—I can't stay in a world where I'm dead.

I reach a familiar corner, but it's not the one I'm looking for, not yet. I glare up at the street sign to figure out how far I still have to go, and manage to make out one word: GENESEE.

A snowflake flies directly into my eye. I squeeze it shut, cursing, trying to douse the ice with tears. When I blink again, the route before me looks clearer than anything I've seen all night.

There's a flickering blue TV glow in Nina's upstairs window, which warms something inside me better than any roaring fire. I have no idea what time it is, but somebody here is up.

The bell chimes loudly when I push the button, and almost immediately the faint murmur coming from upstairs is muted. The blue glow stays in the window. I can't bring myself to make eye contact with the tiny peephole, but when I hear the bolt slide and the handle turn, I hold my breath.

She doesn't say anything at first. It's like the first time we sized each other up through the green light. Only this time, she doesn't look at me like I'm dead. And now I realize she must have been there then, holding vigil, the same way I was.

"You were right," I say. "It was Viv."

She brings her hand to her mouth. Her eyes slide over me, slumped against her door frame, half-frozen with no jacket. I don't even want to guess what my face looks like.

"Cam, I'm so sorry." She steps toward me and reaches out, but I move back and she stops. "Are you all right?"

I press my lips together and nod, but I can't look at her.

She opens the door all the way. "Come inside, it's snowing."

I step in and let her close the door.

"Can I get you anything? Tea? A blanket?"

I lean my back against the door and shake my head. "I have to go."

"Yeah." She nods slowly. "You do."

Our eyes finally meet, and I steel myself for her judgment. But what I see in her gaze isn't at all what I expected. There's no I-told-you-so or impatience, no demands to admit she's right. Viv would have worked this situation any way she could. Nina's light brown eyes are filled with compassion, and nothing else.

"I just figured I owe you an apology at least."

"Don't—" she says. "I mean, you don't owe me anything."

I'm not sure what to say next. I gesture to the second floor. "Is Owen asleep?"

Nina glances up the stairs and takes my hand. Silently, she guides me up the steps and down the hall. I get goosebumps thinking of the first morning I spent here. She peeks into Owen's room, holding one finger to her lips. I peer around the corner too, and see him curled on top of his comforter, asleep. A half-empty bowl of popcorn sits on the floor.

"We were watching *Remember the Titans*," Nina whispers.

"Sorry," I say quietly. "I didn't mean to interrupt."

She shakes her head and we drift across the hall toward her room. "It ended an hour ago, but I didn't want to wake him up to tuck him in."

"Good movie." The corner of my mouth twitches. "He's going to be a killer quarterback in a few years."

She smiles tentatively in the dim light. "You think he can?"

"With the right person's support." I catch her eye.

She squeezes my palm. I didn't even realize we were still holding hands. I'm just about to say something, but then she turns on the light in her room.

I blink. It takes several seconds for my eyes to adjust, and several more before I understand what I'm seeing. Ghouls and monsters leer from every wall. *The Creature from the Black Lagoon* hangs next to the closet. Alfred Hitchcock's *Psycho* is by the desk. *Black Sunday* is over the bed. Every poster I saw in the closet now decorates her walls, along with a few new ones, from what I can tell.

"I was always a fan of *Forbidden Planet*," I say, admiring the one by the door.

Nina folds her arms and laughs. "I know."

I turn in a circle. The bed is still made, the desk is neat, and there still isn't a speck of dust anywhere that I can see. But the room is a burst of color. It's full of life—or people screaming for their lives, anyway.

"What made you change your mind?"

"I don't know, I was feeling too much like I did after my parents died, before I met you. Like all I had to do was focus hard enough to make it through life. But after I watched a few of our movies again, I realized I need to have a little fun." She shrugs, smiling at the cheesy, oversaturated gore. "Also, Aunt Car hates them."

I let my eyes travel the room, trying to make this new image of Nina stick. There's a stack of DVDs on the bookshelf, arranged in alphabetical order, corresponding to the posters. "I wish we had time to watch one."

The picture of us at the lake catches my eyes, taped to the mirror.

Nina follows my gaze. "I'm going to miss you. Again."

I take a long look at her, trying to memorize her smooth copper hair, her pale cheeks, her brown eyes, warm and sad. I reach for her, and her face dissolves. We fall into each other's arms. It's so different—comforting and peaceful—not anything like with Viv. I lean my head against Nina's, and her hair smells so fresh. She rubs her hand up and down my back, and we just hold each other. Neither of us speaks.

"Cam, I . . ."

She lifts her head and we both pause for the same second, inches from one another's lips. I hesitate, our eyes meet, and it feels like we're staring at each other across a universe. I close the space and she tastes warm and sweet, like tea with the smallest drop of honey.

Nina is the one who pulls away. She wipes her face. "At least I get to say good-bye this time."

I can't stay. I nod, and walk the few steps to her door.

"Can I walk you there?" Nina says.

I exhale, glad she asked.

"What about Owen?"

She tiptoes across the hall to check him, covers him with a blanket, then turns the muted TV volume back on low. It sounds like the home shopping channel.

"He'll be okay if I come right back," she whispers. "I wish he was awake—to say good-bye."

I touch her shoulder gently. "Maybe this is better. He might think I was a dream."

We creep downstairs and I crack the door to look outside. "It's still sort of snowing."

"Won't you be cold?" Nina asks.

The chill slices its way through my thin shirt and I close the door. "I seem to have misplaced my jacket tonight."

"Hang on one sec."

Nina disappears upstairs and comes back bearing a huge red hoodie with the Rams logo. On the back it says PIKE with my number five in white.

"It's all I have that'll fit," she says. "You can have it back."

"I never had one like this before," I say, pulling it over my head. It smells like her. "Are you sure?"

She nods stiffly, and I can tell she's forcing a smile. "It suits you better than me."

We walk slowly, despite the weather.

I keep trying to think of things to say, but everything that comes to mind seems trivial now. Why bother talking about school, or the future, or anything? What do you say to someone when you know it's your last conversation? What is there to say—besides good-bye?

The snow is lighter now, spitting from the sky one sad flake at a time. We take a left, and the corner comes into view. The street lamp mounted on top of the utility pole filters a pool of yellow light onto the snow-dusted pavement below. I come to a sudden halt, and Nina stops with me. My palms are sweaty, tucked up into the sleeves of my sweatshirt. It's hard to swallow. My leg ought to be aching. Every other part of me is.

"I'm not sure," I say.

"Of what?" she whispers.

"Why do you think this happened? Any of it?"

She shakes her head slowly. "I don't know, it could've just been some fluke in the universe. You missed her, she missed him." She pauses and looks at me. "I missed you."

"But there has to be a *reason*. Otherwise, what's the point?"

I stare straight ahead, thinking of everything that's happened here, and how stepping through that light means leaving all of it, good and bad, behind forever. She grabs hold of my hand and I slide my fingers out of my sleeve, letting them twine with hers.

"Maybe it won't close," I say.

She squeezes my hand, and our eyes meet, but she doesn't say anything.

We walk toward the corner together.

The night is cold and silent. The only sound I hear is our footsteps dragging down the pavement. I focus on our feet so I don't have to see our destination getting closer.

Except Nina's black boots come to a sudden stop. Her fingers tighten around mine.

I look up.

"What's wrong?"

She doesn't answer. She lets go of my hand and walks slowly down the sidewalk. By the way she tilts her head and scans the horizon, it's clear she's listening for something.

"Nina, what?" I ask again.

But then I hear it.

I turn in time to see headlights careen around the corner behind us. The car fishtails on the slick pavement, regains traction, and plows a course straight for Nina. The vehicle passes into the light. It's a deep shade of blue.

I fly the distance between us and crash into her, struggling to push her to safety, but she flails her arms and pushes back, trying to get *me* out of the way. The headlights bear down on us. I can't think or hear over the roar of the engine. It's too late to do anything but plant myself in front of her, close my eyes, and wait for impact.

My heart stops in a squeal of tires.

The world goes silent.

Hot air breathes against my legs, and I crack one eye open. The chrome grille of Viv's car sits inches away from my knees—her headlights cutting me in half. I open both eyes and squint at the smooth front of the vehicle, gasping when I hear my heart still beating in my ears. A short-haired silhouette leans out of the driver's-side window.

"Get out of the *way*, Cam."

"No." A snowflake lands and melts on my cheek.

She hits the steering wheel. "Just—get in the car."

"No."

Nina's breathing is ragged behind me.

A car door slams. The headlights vibrate with the motion. I make out a tall form in the glare, coming toward us around the car. She's changed into jeans and a sweater. Tears shine in her eyes as she steps in front of the headlights.

"Please . . . come with me." Her voice breaks. "We have to go while there's still time."

A heavy tear rolls down her cheek, and I can't help it . . . a small part of me aches for her, even now. "Viv, I'm leaving without you."

She stops and narrows her eyes, uncomprehending, then glances at Nina next to me. One hand moves slowly to her mouth. "With *her*?"

"No." I shake my head. "Just me."

Her face crumples. "You—can't."

"I am."

I look past her to the utility pole on the corner. She follows my gaze.

Her voice quavers. "But I just got you back."

"No, you didn't," I say, turning. "I'm not him, Viv."

She grabs my arm. "I don't care—let me go with you. Please— there's nothing left for me here—"

I pull away until her grip loosens to a tentative touch. I stare at her lank curls, dusted with snowflakes. Her eyes are dark hollows. She sways on the curb, as if the frigid breeze might knock her over. I think of all the choices that were made to get each of us here, all the different ways this night could possibly end. I understand her well enough to know she regrets what she did— on some level. She meant every word when she said she did it because she loved him.

"Let me go."

She stares at me a moment longer, until the disbelief in her eyes goes dim and her hand slides from my arm. She turns away without looking back and gets into the car. The engine revs with a roar that makes my heart skip. The headlights blind me to everything but the sound of the motor and the heat of the grille inches away. Nina's frozen hand reaches for mine, and I force myself to swallow. I listen to the engine idle, and wait, my brain fixating on the rhythmic cycle of the engine until it accelerates with a sudden rumble. I gasp—

The car reverses, backing slowly into the street.

Viv's face is a shadow as the headlights pull away.

I start to exhale, but the blue car keeps reversing diagonally across the road. It moves slower until the brake lights illuminate and it comes to a stop. Under the street lamps, vapor curls from her tailpipe like smoke from the end of a cigarette.

"What is she doing?" Nina asks.

As if in answer, the sound of tires peeling over pavement screeches across the road. The car roars straight for us, headlights switched to bright, blinding me so it seems like she's coming from every direction. Nina's hand tightens in mine, but there's only time for her to pull my arm and cry out.

The engine whooshes past—too close—but not close enough.

It takes too many seconds to blink.

I spot the car careening down the road. She must have missed. She'll come around for another pass.

But she's going too fast—she's headed straight for the pole.

Just like in my dreams, I scream, but there's no sound. I can't look away. I wait for the explosion, glass, fire. There's a shattering impact and a flicker of green.

The car clips the pole, demolishing the side-mirror and the remaining bushes. It skates a sharp arc over the lawn and bumps down into the school parking lot before curving back toward the road.

I step back instinctively, only to find Nina's arms locked around me. I clutch her to my chest. She's staring down the road, one hand over her face. I pull her tighter. We watch Viv's little blue car pull out.

And drive away.

THIRTY-THREE

THERE'S A CANDY-BAR WRAPPER FROZEN TO THE GROUND.
The wooden pole has a layer of dirt below the frost and a new
scar from the impact of Viv's mirror. The bushes look like hell. I
walk straight over and stick my hand out into the dark. It takes
a little fishing around, but eventually my fingers slip into the
familiar electric green a foot or two off the ground. I let out a
breath, relieved.

Nina studies the rocks, the grass, the horizon, looking everywhere but at me. Her face is very serious. She's got on the same
hooded jacket she wore the last time we were here, when she
tried to warn me about Viv. For some reason that picture from
the lake comes to mind. She and I—Nina and Cam—holding
that stupid fish and laughing on a warm summer day. I try to
match up that image with the one in front of me, where she's

bundled in her coat. I can't make out how the summer smile might fit in on her face.

"What if I stayed?" I ask.

"What?" She comes over, shaking her head. "You have to go."

I can't help myself, even though I know she's right. But it doesn't seem fair to say good-bye now, when I'm just beginning to understand her . . . when she's done so much to help me understand myself. A strand of copper hair escapes from behind her ear and I brush it back.

"You could come with me?"

She shakes her head again and smiles wistfully. "Who would make sure Owen gets to be quarterback?"

I sigh, and stare up at the sky, surprised to see a few stars peeking out behind the clouds.

"Do you think they're the same stars?" I ask.

She lifts her chin and gazes up with me.

"I think they're probably the same . . . but different. Like us."

I keep staring until the clouds sweep in again. When I lower my eyes, Nina's looking at me. I usually can't read the tightly controlled expressions on her face, but right now I have a pretty good idea what's on her mind.

"I'm sorry," I say.

She looks surprised "For what?"

"That you lost him." My voice is low. "I know how much it hurts."

She allows herself a hint of a smile and squeezes my arm. "He was a part of my life, however briefly—a happy part."

"There's something I've been wondering . . ." I hesitate, stepping closer. "If it's okay to ask?"

Nina shrugs and raises her eyebrows.

"What did the note mean? 'You saved my life'—in your yearbook?"

She looks down at the sidewalk and presses her lips together.

"I don't know," she says after a moment.

"But you must have some idea . . . why would he write that?"

"I wish I knew." She shrugs again and lets out a long breath. "He wrote it that night—before it happened. I didn't see it till he was gone. I never got to ask."

I take her hand, recalling the cruel way I'd rubbed those words in her face.

"I didn't know."

She raises her head. "On good days I thought maybe it had something to do with Viv. He'd just broken up with her; he realized she was trouble." She swallows hard. "On bad days I thought it was some awful premonition. One I didn't figure out in time."

A tear escapes down her cheek, and I pull her close, tucking her head under my chin. I try to put myself in his place, figure out what he must have been thinking, but I keep coming to the same answer.

"I can't tell you for sure," I whisper. "But I know you saved mine."

We both hold on a little longer than necessary, but when she pulls away, her hint of a smile is back. She meets my eyes and I catch a glimmer of something—a lake, the sun. Just a flash of memory she keeps, alongside many other things.

She kisses my cheek. "Thanks."

We both turn toward the pole. But this is happening too fast. I'm not ready to leave—not just yet.

"You'll still go to England, won't you? To your mom's little town?" If I never see her again, I want to know what she'll be doing.

"Of course," she says. "Not just to visit—someday it'll be home."

She puts a warm hand on my shoulder, and I know I have to go.

"Tell Owen I'm rooting for him," I say.

"I will," she whispers.

I squat and try to gauge the sliver of green I have to fit through. It's going to be tight. I sit down and stick one heavy foot in. I just have to do this or I'll never go. My toes tingle through my shoe. I turn sideways and slide the other foot in. I work in up to my waist easily, half-transparent and body buzzing, but then I get hung up.

"Your sweatshirt's caught," Nina says, kneeling.

I feel around where I'm stuck, and she's right.

"It's too big for me anyway." I slide it over my head and hand it to her. She grabs hold of me as I pull away.

"Take it with you, it's yours."

I shake my head. "You keep it. It isn't mine to take."

I give her hand a light squeeze and let go, sliding further into green oblivion. She flattens herself on the ground in order to see me, looking worried.

"Are you sure it still goes all the way through?"

I wiggle my feet to check. The space is so tight I can't look down to see my toes, but the pins and needles in them are dissipating, and I can feel the frozen grass on the other side.

"No place like home," I say.

I edge in the rest of the way, and the energy envelops my head. I look back out at Nina through the green filter, the way she looked when I first saw her. She covers her mouth.

"Good-bye, Cam," she says suddenly, reaching into the void to touch my hand.

Both of us are pressed flat with our chins in the dirt. I take her hand and squeeze it one last time. "Good-bye."

The electric tunnel shifts around me, until it feels like a weight pressing in from all sides. It's hard to breathe. Nina's eyes are wide and afraid. It's shrinking with me inside—I have to move *now*.

I let go of her hand and shove my way toward the other end, working up a sweat despite the frost-covered ground. I edge out backward into the snowy bushes of home. I lift my head and Nina waves from the other side of a void that looks like a flat green window now. I wave back. She smiles. Then my fingers slip out of the field of light, and before I can breathe, she disappears.

THIRTY-FOUR

I'M IN THAT PLACE BETWEEN WAKING AND SLEEPING. THE ONE where everything's still black and peaceful until it gets invaded by my thoughts. I try to block them out, sink back into oblivion with no consciousness and no dreams. But eventually I open my eyes, wincing like someone who's been underground. I've been trying hard not to keep track of the days since the green light vanished.

The sun streaming in my window says it's late, but my phone says it's Sunday. I pull the sheet back over my head.

My door bursts open and Mom barges into the room.

"I made you an appointment with Dr. Summers tomorrow. This has got to stop."

"What?" I sit up. "Mom—"

She crosses her arms, flustered. "Look, I don't know what

happened this week—you were doing so well. I thought you were finally dealing with what happened to Viv—"

If she only knew. I roll to face the wall.

"Your appointment's at four, Cam, *tomorrow*." She hesitates. "If you want to argue, call your dad."

Dr. Summers folds her hands in her lap.

"It sounds like things are going pretty well with your dad and school. I thought for the rest of today you might want to talk about Viv?"

I shift in my seat and glance at the clock, but we're only fifteen minutes in and I've already exhausted every safe topic. The truth is, I've been dying to talk to her about losing Viv *again* all weekend. But I haven't come up with a way to do it that doesn't sound insane. I rest my elbows on my knees and rub my temples, trying to clear my head. I may have left Viv behind physically, but she's been invading my mind with a vengeance. Like a part of her still won't let go—or is it a part of me?

"It's not that I don't want to talk about her . . ." I say, off to a brilliant start.

Dr. Summers doesn't say anything except "I'm listening" with her eyes.

I struggle to find the right words. "I'm just not sure our relationship was always what I thought . . ."

"How does it seem different to you now?"

I look out the window. This is the part I'm hung up on, but I can't exactly ask how two versions of the same person can seem so different—and, I'm starting to realize, so very much the same. In both worlds, Viv was needy, but intensely devoted. She was also used to getting what she wanted. Suggesting I didn't need football after my injury made sense to her. It was a window of opportunity—she could become my whole world. What didn't compute is the thought that I'd ever refuse. It scares me that the two versions of her are starting to seem like the same girl. But I'll never know how *my* Viv would have reacted if I'd made a different choice.

"I *did* love her . . . and I know she loved me," I say without looking up. "I've just been thinking a lot about how things were, and how they could've been. But it's stupid because it's not like I can change anything."

"It's hard not to second-guess yourself." Dr. Summers nods. "But the choices we make now help inform the future."

I look up. "How am I ever supposed to know the *right* way to choose?"

"Sometimes there is no right or wrong," she says calmly. "Sometimes you just have to go with your heart."

THIRTY-FIVE

I'VE DECIDED THE BEST WAY TO GET MOM OFF MY BACK IS employment. I walk out of the mall with a few business cards and a stack of generic applications to fill out. Apparently everyone already hired seasonal help for Thanksgiving, but it doesn't hurt to have a desperate teen up your sleeve in the month of December.

I spot Mike's rust-red Toyota coming around the side of Macy's. He flashes his lights when I wave. When he pulls up, some terrible indie rock music is blasting from the speakers.

"Did you put in a subwoofer or something?" I strain to be heard over the noise.

He turns the volume down. "You noticed."

I get in, but my rib cage vibrates even with the sound turned down. "Your dad finally cough up the money or what?"

"I bet him I could win this art contest. Managed second place."
He slides a drawing decorated with a red ribbon off the dash and
hands it to me.

I recognize it as the one he's been sketching for weeks and my
stomach sinks. I'm certainly not getting any awards for friendship lately.

"Wow, man, congratulations."

He stares straight out the windshield and puts on his blinker.
"So, I'm just taking you home, right?"

I hesitate, looking at the picture. "Actually, you hungry? Want
to grab a bite?"

"I kind of have some things to do."

He revs the engine, though the light in front of us is red.

"Okay, I'm sorry. I know I've been a total dick," I say. "I was
just thinking we could do something . . . maybe go to the chicken
place?"

He raises his eyebrows, but stays focused on the intersection.

I shift in my seat, recalling our last trip there, when he had
to drag me out the door. But then I think of Nina in her green
apron.

"Look, remember when I asked you to cover for me, and you
said I owed you an explanation?"

"Yep." The light changes and he turns the wheel toward the
little country diner.

I glance at the stars coming out in the sky.

"How about I buy you dinner instead?"

* * *

Dina's Delicious Diner isn't as packed as the last time we were here. Mike asks for a booth, and my heart goes from adrenaline-infused to full panic mode.

I don't see her anywhere.

A rooster greets us at the table—the same one as last time, I think.

"Is it bad that I've actually been kind of craving that poutine stuff since last time?"

"Actually, that sounds good, I'll have that too," I say, standing abruptly. "I'm . . . going to wash my hands. Be right back."

I walk across the restaurant, eyeing the front doors. I don't know what I'm doing here. I should leave. Even if she's here, I know it isn't *her*—

I stop.

She's standing behind the counter.

I watch her take an order over the phone. She's writing on a pad and smiling. Hair tied back, green apron. I stare at her mouth and marvel at her carefree expression.

"Okay, Mom, I got the order, don't be ridic—yeah? Well, tell Owen that if he survived practice, he can wait twenty more minutes!" She laughs. "I gotta go. See you guys when you get here." She hangs up and shakes her head.

"Nina?"

I cringe as soon as I say her name. She doesn't *know* me. . . . Then I have a worse thought: Maybe she'll remember me from last time.

"Hi," she says, clearly trying to place my face.

"Sorry—you don't know me. I read your name tag."

"Oh." She touches the plastic pin on her apron and smiles hesitantly. "Can I help you?"

I blank. What do I say? My face heats up. Why am I even here?

"Application!" I say. "I mean, um, I was wondering if you had one? I've been looking for a job."

"Oh!" She reaches under the counter and pulls out the same generic form I swear is used by every minimum-wage job in town. She slides it toward me with a pen. "You can fill it out now, if you want. I think we're hiring dishwashers."

I hesitate. Her tone seems too light, but the warmth in her voice is familiar and sets me at ease. I fill out the page with all the same boring information I put on the others. I'm not sure what I think will come of this. She might not even like me, but if there's a chance we could even be friends . . .

"Uh, here you go," I say.

Our fingers touch when I hand the completed form back to her, and I get this sensation, not like a tingle or shock, but something about it is electric. Her pen falls to the floor, and I retrieve it, but when I stand up, there's something curious in her eyes. Did she feel it too?

"Great, thanks . . . Camden Pike." She glances at the page and smiles, holding out her hand. I stare at first, forgetting this strange human custom, but then my brain snaps back to life and I take her hand in mine for the first time—again. "Nice to meet you," she says. "I'm Nina Larson."

ACKNOWLEDGMENTS

THE FORCES THAT MUST COME TOGETHER TO TURN A HINT OF AN IDEA into a debut novel are considerable and something I marvel at every day. Here are a very few of the many people who made this book possible:

Courtney Summers and Tiffany Schmidt, for having the most opposite, frustrating, and discerning opinions anyone could count on from two critique partners. And for becoming two of my closest friends despite this whole crazy process. Courtney: WWIDWOC? Tiffany: Have I told you you're pretty?

My agent, Mary Kole, for being a more enthusiastic advocate of my work than I ever dared to be. Taryn Fagerness and Michelle Weiner, for literally taking this book places I never dreamed. Special thanks to the Andrea Brown Literary Agency.

My fabulous editor and publisher, Alessandra Balzer, as well as

Donna Bray, Sara Sargent, and the entire talented and insightful staff at Balzer + Bray and HarperCollins, including Emilie Polster, Stefanie Hoffman, Brenna Franzitta, Caroline Sun, Olivia deLeon, Molly Thomas, Patty Rosati, Ray Shappell, Erin Schell, Alison Donalty, and Ruiko Tokunaga.

Trespassers William and DJ Encore, whose music inspired and brought my characters alive in incredible ways. Alexandra Sophie, for a gorgeous cover photograph.

My husband and best friend, Stefan, for putting up with endless sinks of dirty dishes and so much more. Mom and Dad, for never saying a discouraging word and for jumping up and down when good things did happen. My sister, Charlotte, and her husband, Mike, for giving me some of the very first feedback I really needed to hear.

Additional huge thanks to everyone who inspired, advised, read, or simply encouraged me along the way: Louise Martorano, Matt Lowery, Jodi Bova, Gillian Perry, Susan Adrian, Linda Grimes, Scott Tracey, Victoria Schwab, Brenna Yovanoff, Nova Ren Suma, everyone at Verla Kay's Blueboards, Stephen White and Rose Kauffman (and Abbey), Eva Barkman, every single encouraging, understanding former Shampoodle client, and the unstoppable Apocalypsies, for their tidal wave of support and enthusiasm all year.

Thank you all.